A Woman's Love and Protection:

A Binding Contract with Life and Death

Lady Donna Thomas

This title is intended for the enjoyment of adults, and is not recommended for children due to the mature content it contains.

First published 2024
by Rowanvale Books Ltd
The Gate
Keppoch Street
Roath
Cardiff
CF24 3JW
www.rowanvalebooks.com

A CIP catalogue record for this book is available from the British Library.
ISBN: 978-1-914422-85-0
Hardback ISBN: 978-1-914422-84-3
Ebook ISBN: 978-1-914422-86-7

The family are tucked up in their beds, fast asleep. They live in a four-bedroom house with a swimming pool and music room. They are a rich family, but they aren't snobby or stuck up. They are very well liked and always have friends and parties, and they help others if needed.

David is the headmaster of a comprehensive school. Marie is still in the army. They have other jobs outside of school hours, to earn more money. Marie loves her martial arts and biking, her dragon duvet covers and pillow set. The heart of a wolf, soul of a dragon. Her office is full of martial arts trophies. Pictures of her and her team with the vehicle mechanics in the army. Her elder son is into motorbikes, as they are a biking family—except their dad. Her second boy is into *Transformers*. Her young girl loves *Frozen*.

Marie met David when she was training in Scotland. They met in the pub, playing darts and pool. She was the only one sober and had to get her men back to the base after a few too many drinks. One by one, she carried them over her shoulder to the vehicle. David gave her a hand, and they got talking. They would meet each other when she was off duty.

The children come running into their bedroom and jump on the bed to wake them up. They fall on them to get them moving; the parents groan a little. Marie hits them playfully with a pillow. The children hit their parents back. David grabs their legs and pulls them down and piles them up and holds them.

It is Saturday morning, and Dyffryn's seventh birthday. The children get to choose what they want to do on their birthdays, but their parents will still tease them.

Dyffryn:
Get up, get up! Both of you, get out of bed now! Come on, it's time to go.

Marie:
What do you mean, it's time to go? Go back to bed, it's too early to get up.

Kyle:
It's her birthday and you know it. Now get up, both of you.

David:
Birthday? There is no birthday. All birthdays have been cancelled until further notice.

Justin:
Ok, let's do this. Mam first, Dad last. Remember the song 'Three in a bed and the little one said...'

Dyffryn:
Roll over!

And the children push Marie off the bed and onto the floor. They all laugh. Now it is David's turn. He wonders if they are even strong enough to push him out of bed. They work together again and eventually push him off. David and Marie sit at the bottom of the bed.

David:
Ok, you got us up—and our attention. What are we doing? Where are we going? Where do you expect us to take you?

Dyffryn runs to the wardrobe and pulls out two boxes from the bottom. She holds up a shoe from each box—ice skates! Her face glows with excitement.

Marie:
No—think of something else to do. We're not good at ice skating, tup.

David:
Sorry, I'm with your mother on this one. We're too old for the cold now. Ask your granddad. He will be happy to take you. We forgot how, anyway.

Justin:
Nice try. Now who is being tup? Besides, Granddad's even older than you, Dad! Get your skates on and we'll meet you in the car. Don't be long.

David:
(to Marie)

Why ice skating now? Where has she got that from? How does she know about our skates?

Marie:
There are no secrets with the kids, you know that. They go through everything. They must have found them looking for Christmas presents? She likes Frozen, Dancing on Ice... You'll have to find your camcorder and record them.

David:
Top of the wardrobe.

Marie:
Oh, very funny.

David:
Well, I thought it was. We'll just have to stretch you a little bit.

David puts a necklace around her neck, one that he bought her. A blue heart with diamonds also in the shape of a heart, with writing on it. *I love you forever*. She loves it: a lovely gift, and a surprise for her.

I love you forever

They walk down the stairs and check with each other, making sure they have not forgotten anything before they leave for the morning. David helps Marie put her black fur coat on.

David:
You drive like a madwoman. I'd like to get there in one piece.

Marie:
I've given Lucy and Kieran my house key. They'll bring the party food and Dyffryn's friends. I've texted Dad to meet us at the ice rink. Have we got everything?

David:
Skates, cam, wallet, phone, house key, they have car keys. I think that's everything. After you.

Marie:
No, you need to warm the pool water up for the children. They'll want to get in as soon as we get back.

David:
I'll be right back, hold on.

He comes back and, as always, is a perfect gentleman. He carries the bag and opens the door for her. He likes to walk behind her, likes to stare at her arse. He walks around the passenger side and opens the car door for her and closes it once she is in. Then he gets in the car himself.

Marie:
Is everyone strapped in back there? Dad's not going anywhere till you do.

Justin:
All present and correct.

David:
Justin, change places with your brother, please. I can't see out the back window with your head in the way. The rate

you three are growing, your mother will have to start sitting in the back. *(Marie hits him)* Ow! That hurt.

The boys get out and change places, and buckle up again.

Kyle:
Ok, Dad, ready to go.

They pull off and are on the way. The radio plays in the car with a little music, not too loud. They are nearly there when Marie's phone makes a noise and a message comes through. Everyone looks at her for her choice of ringtone—it's a little creepy as it repeats over a few times. '*Mammy, mammy, mammy.*' The message is from her father, saying he has arrived there. Then the phone rings with a new ringtone: *'I see you; I see you.'*

David:
Was wondering what the hell that was for a second there. How creepy that sounds—especially starting off.

Marie:
I know, I changed it. It's Dad calling.

She answers the phone.

William:
(on the phone)

Time of arrival?

William Thomas, Marie's father, hates it when people are not on time or early. He likes to get every second he can with everyone; he's not getting any younger, and he loves to make the most of life. He loves doing things with the children for their birthdays. Every year is different.

Marie:
Hi, Dad. We are about five or ten minutes out. David is driving.

William:
I'll meet you inside. Tell him to stop being a snail and shift his arse. I'll see you when you get here, hun.

Marie:
Bye, Dad.

Kyle:
Dad Bill is joining us!

Marie:
Yes, he is. You know he does not miss out on your birthdays. He can help teach you skating.

David:
Ok, here we are. Justin, take care of your brother and sister.

They've arrived nice and early with no one else around. The morning sun is bright and blinding. David gets out of the car and walks around to open the passenger side door. He offers his hand, and Marie takes it and gets out. He shuts the car door and grabs the bag from the boot of the car. He takes hold of one of Dyffryn's hands while Marie takes the other.

William is already on the ice waiting for them. David sorts out shoes for his children. They all sit down on a bench together. David sits his daughter on his lap and helps her with her skates. David goes on the ice first, and then he and William both help the children and Marie. The children hold on to the side. They are excited, waiting to laugh at each other, hoping the others will fall first.

Justin:
This is not as easy as it looks.

David:
We did say to choose something else. Blame Tup here for today. But you're here now, so make the most of it. You are going to have to let go of the side one at a time.

Marie starts the camcorder.

William:
Justin, come with me. Your dad can help Kyle. Dyffryn, stay with your mother for now.

David:
Keep your back straight, knees bent. If you lean too far forward, you will fall over. Legs apart slightly more. I will pull you first—watch my feet and how I move. Then you will do the same. And keep hold of me for now!

William:
Most important thing is how to stop. Use the side of your blade, like this. Now you have the basic movements.

Justin and Kyle try a few times and fall over, landing on the cold ice, careful not to cut themselves with the blades on their feet. David helps them back up by offering his hand, and then his sons take it. Normally, parents grab their child's wrist or arm and pull. Instead, David meets them halfway by offering help. It shows that he cares, but it's his sons' choice whether to accept his help or to get up by themselves. Either way, they know their dad's there for them.

When they fall, the children try not to bang their heads on the ice, tucking their chins into their chests. They use their hands to fall and get back up, like they have been trained to do in the dojo. They're not scared of getting hurt. They know falling is expected and part of life, and getting back up is what matters. The parents don't laugh at them but support them. That way they are never afraid and never stop trying; they keep going and have fun with it.

After fifteen minutes each, the boys are up and going with the basics and are sent to skate around the rink. They practise while it is the ladies' turn to learn. Dyffryn, wearing a helmet on her head for safety, is with her father, and Marie is with her own father. Marie is enjoying the time and remembering her childhood as if it was only yesterday, only now her father needs some support to stand. William might not be able to lift her anymore, but he can still skate with her and hold on to her, just spending time together. It's not about what you can and can't do anymore; the enjoyment is in being there, the love and fun is still there in this precious time together, still making good memories.

David skates up to his wife and switches partners to dance. David and Marie lose track of time as they are having too much fun. Marie loves being in the arms of her loving husband, dancing together, making each other smile. He still has the strength to hold her while doing some lifts, catching the attention of his children. Marie and David are smiling. They had forgotten what it is like to do things together, always with the children while the other watches.

Dyffryn skates up to her father and changes partners. Marie smiles at her and skates to the side. David takes her skates off her feet and skates around with her, doing easy lifts holding her, careful not to hurt her. Dyffryn is having the time of her life. She is such a daddy's girl.

At the end, David skates back to the side with his family. Dyffryn is not happy putting her shoes back on. She just wants to stay all day. They head home with the boys in William's car.

They all arrive at the house. Marie, with Dyffryn in front of her, walks in first. Entering the living room, Dyffryn jumps out of her skin in surprise. Lucy, Marie's sister, is holding a birthday cake in her hands, the candles burning.

Everyone:
Surprise! Happy birthday to you. Happy birthday to you. Happy birthday, dear Dyffryn. Happy birthday to you!

Lucy:
Blow out the candles and make a wish. Deep breath and go. *(Dyffryn blows out the candles)* Time for presents, I think. Here you go, tup.

Dyffryn starts to open all her presents from her friends, from clothing to games and DVDs. Her parents hold off till later. Dyffryn stacks all the presents in a corner of the room to play with later. The children all race for the bedrooms to get changed, then head to the pool. David sorts out the music for them out there as they dive and jump in, splashing each other. He throws them a ball to play with, then goes back to join the others, leaving them to it. Kyle and his friends are playing Twister in the living room. Justin and his friends are in the garden putting up tents. Back in the kitchen, the adults have gathered around the table. The men are in the living room talking and waiting for their drinks.

Marie:
Dad, can you reach the glasses in the top cupboard please? The beers are in the fridge. Lucy, if you sort out the others with wine. Thanks, Dad.

Marie is William's favourite daughter, and he is very protective of her. She always made other children uneasy in school and only had a few friends, so she tried to hide herself from others and be the silent one. Marie keeps those thoughts from her mind, with her friends being there right now.

William:
What are you drinking, sweetheart?

Marie:
I'm still on orange juice. Thanks, Dad.

Her friends look curious; she normally drinks at events. She only drinks soft stuff when dieting and training or pregnant. The women look at each other and then at her.

Claire:
Not pregnant again, are you?

David walks into the kitchen with the other guys, only catching Claire's last statement. He's curious. Not wanting to jump to conclusions, he makes sure to get the story right first.

David:
Who is pregnant again?

Stacey:
Marie, because she's only drinking orange juice. And she's eating pickled onions—everything that goes with pregnancy!

Marie:
No, I am not expecting. Just trying to be careful of my weight and size, that's all.

David laughs at the last part of that, nearly choking on a piece of cheese.

Natasha:
You can skip one day and have a drink with us. Lucy, a glass for her.

Marie gives in and has a glass. She knows she can always work it off later. David walks up behind her and stands with his arms around her.

David:
I love the way you look. You don't need to diet or worry about your weight. You do not need to lose any more—I'll have nothing left to grab hold of. I know I tease about you being small, but I'm joking. I love you that way.

Graham:
What do you mean? She's short, but she's got big enough tits to grab hold of—doesn't matter if she's fat or thin. Not that I'm calling you fat, Marie.

David stands behind Marie with his hands covering her boobs as he holds them firmly, making Graham, whose wife has no boobs, a little jealous.

David:
More than a handful is a waste. She's got a great pair.

David is not happy with Graham after that remark—he should not be looking at his wife. He tries to brush it off with jokes, not to ruin a birthday. A grown man should know better. David puts an arm around Marie and kisses her before walking away. Graham gets hit by his wife Stacey for the remarks and making her feel uncomfortable. They all walk to the living room and get settled as Kyle and his friends take their game of Twister to the bedroom. Watching the children leaving gives Steven a thought, and he has to open his big mouth.

Steven:
I don't know what the fuss is about having children. I've got two, and women always make it out like they're in hell when they give birth. You're just bad with pain, you women, that's all.

William:
Us men have it easy. Women do go through hell and pain. They definitely are not weak, having to give birth to us, and teasing them will only get you into trouble.

Mark:
I'm with Steven. There is nothing we can not deal with better. If that was us, we would breeze it. We work hard at pain, just like working on our bodies and keeping our six packs.

Graham:
If it really was as bad as they say, we would only have one child, not five.

The women sit there with grins appearing on their faces as they think, *Be careful what you wish for—you might actually get it.* Stacey gets a plan and starts to stand up.

Stacey:
I'll be right back, just getting something from the car.

Natasha:
You guys are about to find out for real. William, you are going to enjoy watching this lot squirm.

Steven:
Stacey has the devices in her car, I bet, the ones that make you feel like you're in labour. I've heard of them. We'll breeze them, if that's what you're planning there.

Lucy:
You'll soon find out, once Stacey gets back.

David:
Hold on. I am not getting involved in this. I'm not one for pain at the best of times. I already know she went through hell—I nearly lost her to all three of our children. Count me out.

Stacey comes back in with five devices for them all. Her heart is racing with excitement. The children are still in the pool, out of earshot of all the screaming that is about to start.

Natasha:
I can't wait to see your faces, all five of you.

Stacey:
Ok. I'll put them on you all to make sure they're on right, so you men can't try and cheat by pretending they are on.

Stacey starts with her husband Graham, then Steven, Mark, Kieran, and finally David. The men all think they can breeze it easy, except David. He is dreading everything to come.

Marie:
Right, guys, I'd want to lie down for this if I were you. David, you take this settee. Steven, you take that one. Rest of you, on the floor.

Claire and Steven are married, so they're paired together, with her operating his device. So are Stacey and Graham, Natasha and Mark, and Marie and David. Lucy's with her brother Kieran. Stacey starts the machines. The boys look at each other. They have no idea what to expect, except David. The settings keep changing and their faces start to change with it as their muscles tense. Each guy has a different threshold; some struggle and do not want to do the rest of the settings. They wanted to do this—wanted to prove how tough they are—and now they are paying the price for it. The screaming and swearing have started. The women try so hard not to laugh but can't help it. They remove the devices once they have finished, and the men just lie there in so much pain, glad it's over. They can't move, and don't want to.

Mark:
Jesus fucking Christ, how the fuck can you women go through that?

Steven:
No wonder you crush our hands.

Graham:
I always get, 'Touch me ever again and I'll have yours cut off.' Jesus Christ, it still hurts after. I don't want to move.

David:
Fuck's sake, that really hurt. Did we really have to go through that to prove it to them? Stacey, I can't believe

men actually go to your place of work and put themselves through that before having children with their partners.

Stacey:
I found those that come and go through it, their relationships last longer, they respect and love their partners more and support and help their partners more. Their ego and attitudes change. They calm down and grow up and mature more with their partners.

Mark:
I agree with that—anything not to have to go through that again!

Kieran:
I can see why only Marie has had more kids than you, and why Lucy keeps clear of guys. I definitely respect my partner more now.

Marie:
Ladies, we will leave the men here to recover. We can fill up our glasses and talk in the kitchen.

Graham:
Do you think it makes any difference when they give birth in the water pool?

Steven:
I don't think so? One of mine was born that way. Looked the same to me.

David:
All three of ours were born in the water pool. She finds it helps after the birth. For her, I think it's more about feeling clean from the blood and it helps soothe, like a bath. *(He groans in pain.)* Next time you guys open your mouths, I will fucking shoot you.

The women are laughing their heads off, listening to them talk. William leaves the room in stitches, tears in his eyes from laughing so much. He joins the ladies sitting around the kitchen table.

William:
That was priceless. If your mother was here to see that… I kind of feel sorry for them. David got roped in on that one. I do feel sorry for him—I thought you might have been lenient, with his age against him.

Claire:
Talk about screaming the house down. How is your new job going, Marie?

Marie:
So far so good, the phone hardly stops. I hate having to lie to him about where I am going.

Natasha:
It's a shame; he should be supporting you with your dreams. You don't stop him doing what he wants.

William:
Show them your website and your photos on the discs. Your laptop is here somewhere—I moved it, not to spill drinks on it. Here you go, in your bag.

Dyffryn comes running out of the pool and into the living room. She's not sure what to think of what she finds in there, but is a little worried about her father. Seeing the others, she knows he's not ill.

Dyffryn:
Dad, Dad, some of us are thirsty. We need help to get the ball, it is stuck in the net. Dad, are you ok? Why are you all lying on the floor? (*Shouts.*) Mam! Something's wrong with Dad and the others!

David:
Ask your mother or Dad Bill for help. Don't shout—ask your mother to bring in some drinks for us. You know not to come in here soaking wet.

Dyffryn stands there for a moment, looking at them strangely. Why are they lying there like that? She walks to the kitchen, head down.

Dyffryn:
Mam, Dad wants drinks. Granddad, can you help me get the ball down, please? I think Dad and the others are drunk. They are on the floor. They look like they are in pain.

William:
Your dad will be fine. I'll take care of them first then get the ball. Your friends trying to tease you by balancing the ball up on the hoop again? Where is Justin? He could have helped you—he's tall enough to reach.

Marie:
I had them putting up tents in the garden. Probably finished now and up in their room playing video games? The girls can sleep in our room. Kyle's friends can sleep in his and Justin's room. Justin and his friends are sleeping in the tents. We will sleep in the living room.

William takes care of David and others with drinks first, then gets the ball out of the net in the pool room for Dyffryn. He takes drinks for Kyle and his friends, who are watching *Transformers* films in the bedroom. Then he walks to the garden, where Justin and his friends are in a tent. They climb out to take their drinks, hiding the entrance behind them. They watch William leave and walk back into the house with a smile on his face.

Steven:
I have a question to ask. What is it with Marie and birthday and Christmas presents? She always gives two presents, and one's always a sex toy!

Mark:
Yeah, does she think we go through that many of them or what?

Graham:
Are all those dildos and vibrators a hint we should use them, because you do or something?

David:
(*laughing*)

We don't use any toys. It's a joke with her every time. Someone was not happy with the present she got them once, so since then, she gives a sex toy as well—so if you don't like the first present, you can go fuck yourself.

Graham:
David, you never did say how you got lucky with marrying a younger woman. Twenty years difference. Just looking at your wedding photos. How did you know she was the one?

Mark:
Loads of us would love to have a younger model on our arm. (*He looks at the photos*) How the hell can you wear a kilt? Looks good though. Got to be in hot weather—can't see you doing it in the cold.

Steven:
I bet she's really good in the sack. What did you do, to get her wanting to stay with you?

David:
One never speaks of what happens in the bedroom. When I met her in the pub, and I laid my eyes on her for the first

time, I felt like we already knew each other. Love at first sight. I knew then she was the one for me. She was helping her people back to the military vehicle. I took the chance to help and talk to her. I saw her there again a week later. I joined her and got chatting, and here we are. We were all in kilts for the wedding—it's a tradition with our families for weddings and events. Besides, I think she fell for my charms and good looks.

Graham:
More like you're tall and can reach where she can't, being a short-arse. Women are always cold; they love to stick their cold hands and feet on us to warm up. Back to the kilt thing, it's what we call easy access—walking around a corner and lifting the skirt, or bent over the table. I know I would not be able to keep my hands off for long. I don't mean you in a kilt—it's my wife and her skirts or dresses. David, are you ever going to shave off your beard and moustache? Time for some change. We are curious what you look like without it.

Mark:
(*to David*)

I think you like a woman in uniform. Army photos. Martial arts uniform. Biking clothes in leather. Wonder if she has a kinky side to her? Sorry, change the subject. I'd like to keep my teeth and nose in place.

Graham:
(*looking at a photo*)

She's in a bikini here. Does she have many tattoos? I've only ever seen the Chinese dragon head on her arm.

David:
Body piercings are what I like—I'll say no more. Marie does not like me without the moustache. She refuses to kiss me. Even though she loves and prefers me clean-

shaven—she loves the smoothness. I surprised her once and shaved it off. I blindfolded her; she only kissed me once. I had to grow it back. She even kicked me out of the bedroom till I did.

Steven:
Now that is funny. How do you put up with children constantly? Mine drives me up the wall. School and home, school and parties—give us a break! It's nice to have them all in one place and keep an eye on them at the same time.

Graham:
Body piercing... There's no belly button piercing, here. Did she get it done after this or lately?

Graham is staring at the photo, not really paying much attention to what Steven and David are saying. David smiles to himself, not telling them where Marie's piercings are. He thinks of everything that's been said; he doesn't need toys when his fingers and tongue do the same thing. David looks at Steven to answer his question and avoid the other questions Graham might have.

David:
Easy. Hide in the head's office, only see the teachers in the staff room. The only time I see the children in school is at assembly. I only have to put up with mine. They are very well behaved.

Outside, Justin and his mates are piled in a big tent together with magazines of models. They are watching porn on their phones and laptops. The sound is on mute, not to give them away. Marie takes soft drinks and some snacks for them out there. She opens the entrance to the tent, and Justin quickly slams down the lid of the laptop. The boys take the snacks and drinks from her, not saying a thing, red in the face from embarrassment.

Marie walks away with a grin on her face, knowing exactly what they are doing and watching. The boys open the laptop back up and carry on watching.

Hours later, the children are changed into their pyjamas. The girls are watching Dyffryn's new film, *Frozen 2*, in Mam and Dad's room. The boys are watching *Transformers*. The parents are watching a horror movie, *Poltergeist*, and drinking.

Frozen 2 is coming to an end, the credits rolling up the screen. The children can hear what is on the TV downstairs. The girls decide to sneak down and scare the life out of their parents. The children crawl on the floor, not to be seen, and hide behind the settee that Mark and Natasha are sitting on. The girls jump up and put their hands on the adults' shoulders. Natasha screams and jumps up with fright. The children are laughing their heads off, in stitches as they hold their stomachs and ribs. Natasha throws a cushion at them.

Later, everyone has fallen asleep. Airbeds have been blown up for guests staying the night. Kieran is on the settee with his sister. David is on the other settee with Marie fast asleep on top of him. They hold the women in place to be comfortable and warm so they don't fall off. Dyffryn wakes up and goes down the stairs. She climbs up on top of her mother and sleeps for a little bit till she gets cold and wakes up. As she climbs down, she accidently falls on her granddad and wakes him up. He watches as she gets up and looks for some blankets; she wants to keep the people on the settees warm. She drags a blanket across the floor to Kieran and Lucy and covers them. She kisses their foreheads. She then goes to find another blanket and drags it to her mother and father. She tries to tuck them in beneath it. She hugs them and kisses them. William lifts his blanket and smiles at Dyffryn. She gets in with him and goes back to sleep.

The following day, everyone has gone home and the house is clean. Justin finds it hard to look at his parents, knowing that his mother knows what they were watching. Marie just smiles at him.

Kyle:
What are we doing today, Dad?

David:
If it's ok with you, I thought we could all go for a bike ride. We can go to a bike track and take Dyffryn to the skate park, have some fun. Pop to the shops on the way for snacks.

Dyffryn looks at them unhappily—they forgot about her presents! She wonders if her present was the day out at the skating place. Normally they get a day out and a present. Did they forget to get her something?

Dyffryn:
Mam, Dad, what about my birthday present?

It dawns on Kyle that everyone will be going and having fun—except for one of them. It doesn't seem right. He has realised, after all this time, it's always been the case. Until they went ice skating, his mother never joined in the fun with them. She has always been there, but only watching.

Kyle:
What about Mam, Dad? It's not fair on her, watching us have fun. Dyffryn will be in the skate park having fun. We are all doing something—and not her?

David:
One of us has to watch you. I am with you two, Mam will be with Dyffryn. We will have a picnic after for Mam. Mam is not missing out.

Marie thinks it was nice and sweet of her son, thinking of her. Standing up to his dad and telling him straight. But Marie will join in with the children in things she likes doing with them; if not, she likes to watch them. Ice skating, music and dancing together is a family thing. David likes to ride bikes and do stunts—that's more his thing. Marie's thing is more motorbiking and martial arts, which she does with the kids. It works for them.

Marie:
Kyle, it's fine, I don't mind watching you all have fun.
Besides, that's not my sport—I prefer the dojo to the bikes.
Dyffryn, is ice skating and a party not enough?

Dyffryn:
No.

Marie:
David?

David:
Ok, we have got you something. But there's another one
you will have to share with your brothers.

Dyffryn is not happy about sharing her presents with her brothers, but at least she has one that will be all hers and only hers. She is a lot like her mother; she knows what she wants. She is a daddy's girl like Mam; she gets away with a little too much, being the youngest and female—she knows it and uses it.

Dyffryn:
Share first, mine last. What did you get me?

They all head for the music room, where there is a present in the corner. She opens it as fast as she can, all excited. It is a keyboard for her to play with. Her father plays the guitar, her mother the keyboard, drums and the recorder, though she's out of practice—she hasn't played in years.

Dyffryn follows her father to the garage, where the cars and motorbike are. Marie and the boys follow behind. Dyffryn finds a new bicycle with the others. She has her very own bike! David just has to put the stabilisers on for her. Dyffryn is so excited. She pulls the bike away from the wall and looks at it. She tries to sit on it, but the seat is too high for her, so she puts it back against the wall.

They all go back inside and get ready to ride. They pick up their rucksacks, purse, wallet, phones, keys and head off on the bikes, planning to stop by a supermarket on the way.

The five cycle together at a tidy pace, not leaving anyone behind. David leads with Dyffryn on the back, on a flat comfy seat made for her as she holds on to her father. The others follow behind him in a line: Kyle, Justin, and Marie last. It's one way for the parents to keep an eye on the children. Normally Marie would be in front as David likes to be a gentleman, but Marie wants him in front first, so Dyffryn is in the middle with the boys and not behind them all. Not that she doesn't trust him to keep her safe.

Dyffryn isn't happy about not being on her own bike. She can't ride yet, but she thinks it can't be that hard—surely everyone else could have ridden at her speed.

They're all wearing their protective gear: helmets, elbow- and knee-pads. They all know the correct hand signals for turning at street corners or roundabouts. Cars carefully pass them, giving them enough room when passing. Drivers hate having bikes on the road, but bikes are too big and dangerous to pedestrians to ride on the pavement.

They arrive at the shop. David helps Dyffryn off the bike, places the bikes in the bike park and chains them up together, not to be stolen, then they all walk inside to get snacks for the day. They walk through the aisles and pick up everything they need, before they head for the tills. Marie sees Dyffryn run off down the bottom to an aisle that she's seen a person walk into. Marie and David know why. David looks at Marie, who smiles back at him, a way of saying *you go*. David runs after Dyffryn to stop her, catching her just in time. The person in the aisle was a dwarf, a little person, Dyffryn had taken that person for an elf—one of Santa's little helpers! Marie thinks it was funny, but Dyffryn is not happy being stopped and carried back over her father's shoulder.

Dyffryn:
Dad, please! I need to tell her what I want for Christmas!

The boys are laughing their heads off at her. David is embarrassed and just wants to get out of the shop quickly. At last, they pay and leave. They get back to the bikes and David puts Dyffryn down. Marie holds on to her while David unlocks the bikes. David puts Dyffryn back on the seat, and they set off for the bike park.

They all finally arrive at the bike and skate park. Marie watches the boys ride the tracks, and the boys and Dad show off, doing a few stunts. They ride down steps and over walls, dirt tracks and ramps and bridges, through tunnels and a stream, everything a bike rider loves. The boys are getting muddy and fall off a few times. So does David. They are having so much fun. Dyffryn is on her skateboard, practising picking up speed and breaking, watching the other skaters use their feet to kick their skateboards up into their hands. She tries the trick and fails. She starts off on the little ramps, then moves on to the big ones but not from the top. Marie watches her try more a little at a time, building up the speed and balance by starting a little higher up the ramp each time. Dyffryn is feeling pleased with herself. She tries starting a little too high and comes off as she hits the ramp on the other side. When she slides down, instead of crying, she is laughing. Marie is smiling at her, recording her to show the others so David doesn't miss out.

Everyone is getting hungry and they head back to the lawn with the food cabin on site and trees around. They find an area to sit, and David lays the blanket down and pulls out the food and drink. With a smile, Dyffryn sits on his lap. He watches the footage of his daughter. When he goes to move the skateboard to the other side of him, he can see the wheels are a little loose.

A Frisbee lands in front of Kyle. He looks at the lads waiting for him to throw it back. One of them waves his hand to join them, and the children get up and race off into positions. Marie lays her head down on David's lap, and he strokes her hair and kisses her.

Marie:
What was that for?

David:
Does a man need a reason to kiss his wife, show affection and let her know that he loves her very much? If you don't want to be kissed...

Marie:
Not saying that. I love you too. Just... It's been a little while for us to do this. Shame we have the kids with us, that's all.

Marie sits up as they kiss each other. The children spot them, and pull disgusted faces, pretending to vomit. David looks at the boys, all muddy, and they decide to head back for a shower.

They are outside the house with the bikes. David puts the key in the front door, and Dyffryn walks in first, followed by Marie. Marie turns and puts her hand to David's chest, stopping him entering. The boys are looking at her.

Marie:
Not a chance in hell. The three of you can go around the back and take my bike with you. I'll see you at the back door.

Marie closes the front door on them. The boys look at their dad, saying nothing, then look at each other covered in mud. David takes Marie's bike in one hand and his in the other and pushes them both around, the boys following behind. Justin opens the gate for them and they lean the bikes against the shed wall ready for washing. They turn and see Marie standing in the doorway. As they approach her, she picks up towels for them all, but when they go to take them, she pulls the towels back.

Marie:
Right, you three, strip to your underwear or you're not coming in. Put your clothes in that basket for washing.

Justin:
Mam, you can't be serious?

Marie:
Deadly. Ok, you've got the tent to stay in, you need to put it together.

Kyle:
Dad!

David:
No, I know when your mother means it—she means it. Get your muddy clothes off.

Marie:
You too, David.

He is about to say he's not muddy like the boys, when he realises he does have some mud on him from when he came off his bike. He strips to his pants and puts his clothes in the basket. Marie hands them a towel each. David picks up the basket of clothes, takes it inside and puts it all in the washing machine. Kyle goes in for a shower. Marie walks off.

Justin:
Dad, why didn't you put your foot down with Mam? I thought you were the man of the house!

David:
I am the man of the house. One thing you better learn and learn fast, my boy—you never argue with your mother. What your mother says goes. A woman is always right. Learn quickly to say 'Yes, Mam'—or for your girlfriend and wife down the line, 'Yes, love.' Or learn to duck very fast.

Justin:
Even when they are wrong?

David:
Especially then. Look at it this way: if a woman is fifty percent right, you're fifty percent wrong. You want a happy life; you keep them happy. I wouldn't mess with your mother—she is army-trained, I like to wake up in the morning. You can clean the bikes; I'll take Dyffryn out on hers.

Justin:
Yes, Dad.

David takes Dyffryn outside on her bike to let her ride it for the first time. Dyffryn watches her father put the stabilisers on it for her. When she tries it out, she's having the time of her life. David watches her go up and down the street on the pavement with a smile on her face. He smiles back at her. He is fixing the wheels on the skateboard while he watches her ride. The sun starts to go down, and soon everyone is back inside.

Marie walks into the music room to practise on the keyboard. She stops playing when Justin walks in. She gets nervous when people watch her practise. She's afraid of being teased or laughed at, something she never got over as a child who was bullied. David walks in after putting the bike away and joins them in the music room. Marie hands David his guitar so he can teach the boys. David tries to show them how to play a guitar, placing their fingers on it and showing them a few notes to start with. Marie starts off on the drums, but stops to let Justin play and practise. David plays along with Justin as the others watch and listen. Marie then sits down with Dyffryn at the keyboard and helps her to play a Beethoven piece with just her right hand. Not the full version, of course—just bits. She's rusty and is trying to remember it herself. They play for just a few minutes before they go to bed.

Every night, the same routine. David reads Dyffryn the same storybooks: Hansel and Gretel, followed by the Three Little Pigs and the Big Bad Wolf. David gets into bed and cwtches up to his wife, and they fall asleep together after a long day. Half an hour later, Dyffryn runs into their room and cwtches up to them both in the middle. David holds them both, as does Marie. They wait for Dyffryn to fall asleep, then David takes her back to her bed and tucks her in.

They are all finally in their beds, fast asleep. The moon is high in the sky, the stars are out.

The following morning, David and the children are having breakfast together before school. Their mother was not in bed to jump on in the morning. After a good day yesterday, they forgot what kind of hours their mother works. David does get worried about her having too little sleep or none at all; she always makes sure that the children are taken care of first, but her own happiness and health are important. Marie left for a 06:00 start on base. Dyffryn is too young to understand what her mother actually does.

Dyffryn:
Dad, where is Mam?

David:
Gone to work early. Ok, get dressed, brush your teeth and wash. I'll have your breakfast ready soon.

The children leave to get ready, while David sorts their cereal, pours milk or orange juice for them and makes himself a cup of coffee. Kyle comes back down with a note in hand; it was stuck to the bathroom mirror so they would see it. He hands it to his father. Dyffryn runs in behind her brother. David looks for his glasses and finds them next to the microwave. He tries to read Marie's small writing. The note says she has gone to work. To the children, it's not very clear what that means.

Kyle:
Will Mam be back today, or will she be away for months on end again?

David:
It only says she went to work. She has had to go on a training course somewhere? Your mother has terrible writing. So small... good job it's in print. She will be home tonight. I'll drop you off at school and pick you up as soon as I can at the end of the day. Do not go wandering off anywhere after school.

Justin:
Well, we will help with the cooking later. She loves a cooked dinner. She is always cooking for us. She'll be too tired to cook tonight, and besides, it will make a change from the salad she eats every day.

Dyffryn:
She will turn into a little white fluffy bunny rabbit.

David:
Oh Dyffryn, she's already little and white, but I don't know about a bunny. She's more of a little pit bull.

Kyle:
Why is Mam's writing small? It's like ours—why is it not like yours?

David:
She was scared of people reading what she wrote, when she was a kid.

Justin:
Mam, scared? How does that make her writing like it is? It doesn't make sense.

David:
It does if you are being bullied by teachers, not just other children. Your mother was left-handed as a child for writing and eating. Years ago, they used to force you to change hands. Your mother uses both hands, depending on what it is she is doing. Her martial arts gives her a new life, confidence. She made friends. Same with the bikers, a new family, the military—and now us.

The children sit down for their breakfast, while their father leaves to get ready. Justin looks at the note again. He never took his mother as one to be afraid of anything; she seemed the type that you'd be afraid to mess with. He realises, if what his dad said is true, it has made her who she is today, made her strong. A smile appears on his face. She is not a quitter type; knock her down, she will get back up. David walks back in, looking for his laptop to put in his bag to take with him.

David:
Justin, let me know if you need anything for your school trip—your mother usually remembers everything. Pick up what you need on the way home. Are you done with breakfast, and have you got everything you need for today? If so, get your shoes and coat on by the door.

Justin hands his father his laptop from the chair tucked under the table next to him. They pick up everything and leave the house and walk to Marie's car, which is parked right outside the house.

David:
Justin in the front, you two in the back. Looks like she has borrowed my car again.

David adjusts the seat to get in, alters the seatbelt and mirrors. He turns the heating and the radio down. Justin watches him with a grin on his face. David notices it, and starts driving.

Justin:
I bet she thinks the same thing in reverse when you use her car. How come Mam is short? We are all tall.

David:
It's a medical condition. Underactive thyroid. She doesn't let it get in the way of anything she wants to do. She doesn't mention it to anyone—do me a favour and don't mention it yourself either. It's a touchy subject and she went through hell as a kid for it.

Justin:
Ok, I can understand that. Explains the bullying you mentioned, and why she had to take up martial arts to defend herself. And the tablets she takes. Dyffryn found them Saturday night in your room. She thought they might be sweets. She didn't take any, though. Granddad caught her when taking up drinks and snacks for them all.

David:
Thank God for that. I'll move them on to the high shelf in the wardrobe.

Justin:
But then Mam won't be able to reach them!

David smiles at just the thought of it, picturing himself putting the tablets on the high shelf and sitting on the bottom of the bed. Marie would try to reach them on tiptoes, while he'd just enjoy the view of her arse. He loves to wind her up on purpose.

David:
Your mother will, trust me, though she might be small. Dyffryn, honey, listen to me. Please do not touch anything in Mam and Dad's room. You will find no sweets or anything in our room, ok? If you want anything, within reason, ask us. We will give it to you if you are a good girl. But you must not go helping yourself.

Dyffryn:
Yes, Dad. Can we stop for sweets on the way home? Please, Dad. You know you love me.

David:
Now, you know that doesn't work with me. I am not your mother. If you behave, I will think about it. Right, we're here. Let's get you out—big hug for your old man. You can go in with your friends here.

Kyle:
Dad, did Mam leave me money for school dinner?

David:
Yes, she did. It's in your wallet in your bag. Ok, give me a hug before you walk to your class.

Kyle:
Dad, you're embarrassing me—we're too old for hugs now!

David:
Oi, your old man is never too old for a hug from his children! Your mother will always want a hug. Besides, it is my job to embarrass you—it's what dads are for.

Kyle:
It's different from Mam. I just hate it now when she kisses us—I'll be glad when that stops.

David:
Then you've got a shock coming—you better get used to it. When you have a family, you will be doing the same to them. Now get going or you will be late. We all will be late. Make sure your sister is with you when we pick you back up later.

David goes back to the car and drives with Justin to the comprehensive.

Justin:
Dad, you are terrible. You love embarrassing him.

David:
Not as embarrassing as your mother's friend was one year at the school.

Justin:
You got to tell me; you can't stop there.

Justin follows his father into his office, as David is the headmaster. David goes behind his desk and opens a drawer and pulls out a picture of Craig, Marie's friend and colleague, in a green summer dress and sandals, with full facial hair, and hands the picture to Justin. David walks back around the other side of his desk and sits on the desk, looking at the photo with him.

Justin:
That's Craig! What does he look like!? So, what happened?

David:
Craig's daughter, she started skipping classes at school. Craig asked your mother for some advice on what to do about it. I had a shock when he walked through the door. Your mother's answer to the problem is what you hold in your hand. When Samantha saw her father come down the stairs in the dress and flip-flops, she was not impressed and thought he was joking at first. He takes her arm and

her bag and drags her to the car, so I am told. She is crying all the way here, holding her head down trying not to be seen in the back of the car. Craig steps out of the car and opens the back door and marches her inside. Your mother sits on the bonnet of the car, trying not to laugh. She thought he would just stop there and watch her walk in. No, he actually walked her right into the classroom and sat her down in a chair, in front of everyone. He said he will walk her to every lesson, every day for the remainder of her school time here, to make sure she never misses a lesson again, and he will keep dressing like that or worse. He showed her the bra and thong he would wear if it came to it. Everyone was laughing their heads off. Your mother is terrible for stuff like that. It is very effective though. She stopped after that. Never missed a class since.

Justin:
Oh my God, the poor girl. I would have loved to see that. If I know you, Dad, you would do the same to Dyffryn if she started playing up.

David:
Yes, I would. She would have the shock of her life. Your mother has a good sense of humour at times. Right, go and get your mark in class, I will see you in assembly.

The assembly had started and the Lord's Prayer had come around. Justin and his friends had printed off the prayer when they were at the party. They handed it to everyone in the assembly to read aloud. The teachers took their places in the hall.

Assembly:
Our Beer.
Which art in Bottles.
Hallowed be thy Sport.
Thy will be Drunk.
I will be Drunk.

At home as it is in the Pub.
Give us each day our daily Beverage.
And forgive us our Spillage.
As we forgive those who spillest against Us.
And lead us not into poofy Wine Tasting.
And deliver us from Tequila.
For mine is the Bitter.
The chicks and the Footy.
Forever and Ever.
Barmen.

The teachers are shocked, but grins start to appear on their faces as they try not to laugh at the prayer. The children laugh a little and put the print-out in their pockets to take home. David looks at Justin and shakes his head. He's just like his mother. He does find it funny as a father, but has to be strict as it is school time.

Meanwhile, at the army base, they are working on Bedfords, Leylands, Scania and Stalwart trucks. One of the vehicles is about to drop on Marie, but she gets pulled out from underneath just in time.

Craig:
Sorry, that was my fault. Look what we got here! It's our sexy staff sergeant. Come on, strut your stuff up and down this place. Get that sexy body going. We have our very own model here! You should be sprawled over our vehicles in all positions.

Craig is only joking and has a sense of humour. He's not actually hitting on her, they just have a close friendship. No sexual harassment in work—he knows who he can talk to and who not to, he knows what lines he can't cross and not to go too far. He likes having a laugh with Marie.

Marie:
Hey guys, how about doing some modelling of your own? Plenty of vehicles to model in and model on.

Craig:
You kinky bitch. When are you doing the naked modelling? They're the photos we're interested in.

Marie:
Never going to happen. I only model for David.

Craig:
Come on, you can't build us up like that and just stop. Spoilsport. We just had our hopes and dreams come crashing down. But that's ok—you can make it up to me on the first aid course by being my partner and giving me mouth-to-mouth.

Marie:
Yes, ok. Then you can be my partner when I shoot you for target practice at the gun range. I'll bury you at the assault course later.

Craig:
That's fine. I'll die happy. Actually, can we do the assault course first? I can watch your arse go over the walls, bars and ropes again. Ok, going back to work. Just to let you know, I've printed out a few of those pictures and stuck them up on our wall in the office. I just keep the vision of the wall and your arse in mind.

Marie:
We better sort the bridge out and fix the pump.

Marie knows no matter what she says and how innocent it is, it will be turned around into something sexual. She tries for it not to happen and tries to think of different ways to phrase it before speaking, but there is no way around it. It will always be taken that way.

Craig:
You can fix my pump any day. I can open the red flaps for you. Stick in the long pink pipe. There's two hundred and

fifty gallons of fluid to pump through from the bags. Think of all the hard work and sweat we can get on from banging side to side and thrusting everything around. Just picturing it in my head... I'm talking about the bridge and pump house. First a warm wet one, I think. The tea, I meant—you are terrible, Marie! You're totally dirty minded. Not the mouth it comes out of, but the mind it goes into. Yours is totally filthy.

Marie:
Blame me? I am totally innocent! I am a good girl. A little angel, me. I know nothing of what you talk about. Trying to corrupt me...

Craig:
Bullshit. (*Craig coughs as he says the word, putting his hand to his mouth. He nearly falls off a truck*) You're really good at being really bad in that head of yours. Angel, my arse. Angel, yes, I know where your halo is. You are extremely naughty. There's nothing we can say, no matter how innocent it is! You will find it dirty and try not to smile or laugh. You would put *Fifty Shades of Grey* to shame. Just with the looks and laughs you have said it all. When you go really quiet, it's frightening what might be going through your head. Then again, do tell?

Marie:
What, me? Would I do a thing like that?

Craig:
Yes, you would, and you're doing it right now. Shit, I messed that up just now. Can't concentrate because of you. Now I can't even get the rubber out of my trousers. There you go again. Rubber off the pencil. Stuck in my pocket. I can't get it out. Getting further and deeper. It's growing bigger. The hole, that is. In my pocket. I can't get it out. Story of my life. Stop laughing—you're being really rude again. I'm glad the others aren't here listening to this. They'd think we are up to no good here.

Marie:
Why? Do you think they'd help you dig the hole deeper? Do you need a magnifying glass to find it?

Craig:
Funny. My cock is not small either, thank you. Get here and help me with the ball. Hand me the ball cock for the machine, I meant. Jesus Christ, how does David cope with you? You must be hands-on all the time. I meant to get work done, not hands on the body, his body. For fuck's sake.

Marie:
We don't speak like this. Besides, we are more hands-on. He's always got his hands full, in more than one way. He never hears me complaining.

Craig:
Forget helping me with the job, we'll never get it done. I am a dribbling mess; I can't focus with you. Dribbling from the tea. For goodness's sake, women. You are worse than us.

Marie:
Do me a favour while you are working there. I am keeping the wild kittens in there as the mother died. I need you to feed them for me.

Craig:
Feed the pussy. What, the four-legged kind or the other? Ok, I'm going and when I am done, I'll make us a nice wet one. How do you like it—hot with cream or without? I don't take sugar, I'm sweet enough already. Plus, the tea. Sorry, I'm going. I will never see sausage and mash in the same way again.

Marie:
We are as bad as each other. God help us if the others joined in. Outsiders would be embarrassed as we died laughing.

Craig:
The ten of us together—we would die laughing for real, and be buried at the same time. I don't think God or the devil would take us. We'd be kicked out for causing trouble and parties and taking over the place. Keep sending us back with more lives than a cat. Here, pussy, pussy. Hey, just think—if they put us both in straitjackets, the padded cell together would be fun. Then again, if it's just you in the straitjacket, the fun I could have...

They both laugh, and everyone turns up to head out for the assault course. They all get in the truck, and Craig and Marie are last in. She's last on, not to give Craig a chance of looking at her arse getting in. She puts her feet in the holes and Craig offers his hand. She takes it, and he helps her up into the truck. They lift the tail and lock it in place, bang on the truck and head out for training.

Back at the school, a fight breaks out in the yard at dinner time. First year against a fifth year with his friends, always looking to bully someone. James, the bully, flicks a knife in his hand and threatens the young boy, Christopher, pointing the knife in his face. His friends circle around the boy. Christopher is a little nervous.

James:
Hey, where do you think you are going? Give me your money now. What else do you have in your bag we can have?

Christopher:
I'm not giving anything to a bunch of bullies like you.

James:
What did you just say to me? You answering me back? Think you're brave and just going to walk away from us?

Christopher takes a swing at the knife with his bag and kicks James. The group grabs holds of the bag and Christopher, and start beating the crap out of him. The bag breaks, and James goes through Christopher's pockets for money, but he's jumped by Justin and his friends, helping Christopher out. Justin breaks James's nose for him. Teachers break the fight up, taking the main three boys to the headmaster to be dealt with.

There's a knock at David's door, and he opens it to see his boy standing there. He is not happy with what he is seeing, but he is fair; he will listen before judging anyone. James has spent more time in his office than any other student.

David:
Come in, Christopher, James, Justin. Close the door. You three again. What is the problem this time? Why can't you just get along?

Christopher:
They are nothing but a bunch of bullies, sir. They tried taking my money and my bag for school.

David:
Justin, explain yourself.

Christopher:
It's not Justin's fault, sir. He only tried to help me.

James Jones:
Daddy's precious good-doer, can't do no wrong. Pathetic.

Justin:
What is pathetic is you are too scared to fight one-on-one without a knife and friends. Bringing a knife to school, and you still had your arse kicked by me.

Justin hands his father the knife. Christopher's blood is on it, from where the knife cut his hand while he was swinging the bag.

David:
I have heard enough. Christopher, go get checked out by the nurse. Justin, do the same, and both of you, get back to class. James, I am calling your parents to come and take you out of here. You are no longer welcome at this school. You interrupt lessons. Beat every student over every little thing you can think of. You nearly strangled a child to death in one lesson because he wouldn't give you money. You broke the nose and arm of another because he wouldn't give you his dinner, and you threw it over him after it. Molesting the girls… I will not stand for it anymore. Sorry, but we are not doing this anymore. The female teachers are scared of you. Whatever your real problem is, we can no longer help you. We have tried everything. The police and courts will not be bringing you back here anymore.

James:
Sir, there is no other school to go to. I can't get kicked out. They will send me back to juvie, sir. You can't do that; I will not let you do that to me.

David:
You'll find that I can, and I have. You should have thought of that before you got kicked out of all the others. I have responsibilities to other children and the school, not just you. Their safety comes first. The police are on their way to escort you off the property.

James:
I hate you and this school. Never wanted to be here anyway. You all can go to hell. You're a dead man, sir. I will get you for this.

David:
Sit your arse back down. Think you're a hard man with a big mouth and threats? You are just a scared little punk, trying to look big and hard. It does not wash with me. You don't

scare me. You need to grow up. Hopefully you will, fast, where you will be going.

David seals the knife in a poly pocket and puts it into a desk drawer for the police. The children watch from the class windows as a police car arrives and two cops walk in with James's parents, who do not look at all happy about it. One copper takes the knife and the bag. James is handcuffed and carefully put into the car

Meanwhile, Marie is at Army training in Crickhowell. She is practising putting a person into the recovery position. Craig, the corporal, is practising bandaging the arm, leg and head. They finish up, and the instructors pack up the dolls, Annie and Bob. Marie marches the men to the assault course next.

Marie:
By the left, quick, march. Left, left, left, right, left. Left, left, left, right, left.

Within a matter of minutes, they are at the assault course.

Marie:
Halt, left turn. Stand at ease. Four groups of nine, go.

They quickly get together into teams. The first, second and third teams do exactly the same thing: the men go over and under the bars, getting to the wall, which they help each other over. The second tallest goes first with the help of the tallest, who puts his back against the wall and his hands together to give the other a leg up. The first man up grabs the wall, pulls himself up and offers his hand. The smallest is lifted up next, and then the group goes one by one: running the wall, jumping over water ditches, jumping off a wall and rolling, climbing a frame and down a rope on the other side. They laugh and joke, checking the time to see who has done it the fastest. The men range from five foot eight to six foot odd, all in their military uniforms.

Marie is smiling as she does something a little different from the others. She splits her team up again into three groups. Three at one end, three on the other, three in the middle. Marie is on the left. She rubs her hands on her trousers and touches her jacket, as if to get comfortable and dry her hands or get ready. Her hair is in a bun in the net under her beret, she is smiling, looking at the others, focused and off. Three at a time over and under the bars, three at a time over the walls, three running walls used, keeping up and on form. The others watching are not happy—why didn't they think of that?

Marie's group comes to the climbing frame. Three go up. When the first soldiers are dragging themselves across a single bar each at the top, the second goes up the climbing frame. The first are going down the ropes while the second group cross the bar and the third group start to climb. Marie is second. They help each other along the way. Everyone else knows they've lost. Marie let them go first to see what she had to work with. These soldiers can take orders, but they're not yet leaders, need to start thinking out of the box. They shouldn't have to be told how to get over something—one of the groups should have used their brains, and then the rest could follow. She needs a team that will think: it saves lives, not just theirs, but others' too.

School has ended, and the children are all at home doing their homework, while their dad prepares the food to cook. The children walk into the kitchen. Kyle pulls the pans they need out of the cupboard, and Justin fills them with water. Dyffryn picks up a knife off the table. David holds the chopping board with the veg, while Dyffryn scrapes the veg into the pans, adds the salt and starts stirring with her dad's help. The boys grab the rest of their homework to finish it while waiting. When it's time to dish up, the boys get the plates and cutlery.

David:
Slow down, your mother will not eat everything. She's a fussy cow, unlike us. Meat first, roasts on the side. Peas, carrots, sprouts, green beans, Yorkshire pudding. Gravy over it.

Kyle:
That isn't much. Why does she not like the rest? She's missing out on the best bits.

Justin:
She's just not a big eater. Her appetite's like her—not very big.

David:
She calls us greedy cows. Right, sort your own out there. I'll put your mother's in the microwave for later. Dyffryn, wait a few minutes, it will be too hot to eat. Sit at the table tidy, guys. You will help with the dishes—Kyle's turn to wash. Justin can dry and put away. Dyffryn, you can stand on a chair and pass the plates across to your brother to wash. Then you can watch TV with me or play some card games or something, then bedtime.

Justin:
You will have to wash the knives, Dad. Mam will go mad if we do it. They're razor sharp.

David:
The only ones you cannot touch are the samurai swords.

David goes up to the bathroom to wash and get changed into his pyjamas. When he comes back down to join the children before bedtime, they get a massive shock. He has shaved off his facial hair and is now clean-shaven. The boys touch his face to find out how smooth it is and take photos of their father. They can't get over how different he looks. Dyffryn is scared and confused and starts crying when he walks towards her to pick her up. She hides behind her brothers, who are recording her reaction for their mother to see.

David:
Dyffryn, don't be afraid of me—it's Daddy. Don't you like my new look? No? You're like your mother and hate it too. God help me when she gets in, I might be sleeping on the settee again like before.

Justin:
Then why do it, Dad? Dyffryn, it is Dad.

Kyle:
He won't hurt us. No need to hide from him.

Justin:
Dyffryn, where are you going? Give Dad a kiss before going up to bed.

They can't help but laugh. David grabs hold of her and picks her up for his kiss. She starts crying again and is scared and tries to push him away. She really does not realise that it is her dad and not a stranger in the house. She looks around to see if her real dad is hiding to prank her. She goes to her room crying, thinking her dad has left and Mam has a new man in her life. The boys go up to look after her and go to bed themselves.

Marie walks into the house and takes her boots off. She can see he has shaved again. She runs her fingers down his cheek then sits on the settee. David moves in to kiss her, expecting her to move away, but she doesn't. He starts to massage her neck, back and feet, helps her relax after being on her feet all day and running courses.

Marie:
This is really nice.

David:
Feels like you needed it, you've got knots again. How was your day?

Marie:
Please don't stop. Craig saved me from under a vehicle that nearly came down on me. The men will shape up; I showed them something they needed to see. How was your day, babe? How did the children take it?

David:
A good day in general. Only had one problem: I had a student kicked out of school. The kids helped cook dinner for you. They have not long gone to bed. I bet you haven't eaten all day, have you?

David makes cups of tea for them and warms her dinner up. She sits there eating it, smiling away, looking at the cup and trying not to laugh.

Marie:
I wasn't sure if this would be safe to eat—one of you might have poisoned me.

David:
Not sure if I put enough rat poison and arsenic in...

She feels better now she has had something to eat; she always ends up too busy and forgets to eat in the day or doesn't have enough time to do so.

David:
Now you're done, I'm ready for dessert.

He picks her up onto the table, after moving her plate into the kitchen sink. He stands between her legs as she wraps them around him and pulls him in. He moves in slowly to kiss her again. She touches his face and feels the smoothness. He lifts her shirt from her trousers and holds on to her.

Justin walks in to get a glass of water to take back up with him, ruining the moment for them. Both drop their heads and look down as David puts both hands by her side on the table and then looks at his son. Marie smiles at them both. Talk about timing! The joys of having a family. Justin is not happy with what he's walked into. He likes that they still love each other and the family is a family, but hates it when they are about to get it on at home with them around—it turns his stomach. The children find it so embarrassing, especially when their friends are around.

Justin:
Oh please. You will scar me for life. Come on, we've got to eat on that table. We live here too—not something we want to see! So, you won't be sleeping on the settee tonight then?

David and Marie look at each other, David raises an eyebrow at her. Marie smiles back at him.

David:
(*To Justin*)

You've got a room to be in.

Marie:
We can always have you three stay with Granddad or Auntie or Uncle. We'd get the whole house to ourselves.

Justin:
That might not be a bad idea, the way you two carry on here. You got a room for that. Just put a lock on your door, keep Dyffryn out. Speaking of Dyffryn, take a look at this. Her reaction to Dad. Took us a while to try and convince her he is Dad! She's sleeping in my room with me tonight.

They watch the video and laugh; Justin had shared it with his friends on Facebook.

Marie:
Now that is funny. Poor girl. She will have nightmares for life.

Justin leaves the kitchen with a glass of water for him and Dyffryn.

David:
Now, where was I? I remember. Dessert. I love you in uniform. I love you even better out of it. Get that sexy arse up the stairs. Get my hands on that cute little white bum of yours.

A week later on a Wednesday evening, Marie is teaching her martial arts class.

Marie:
Everyone, line up. Justin, start the warm-up please.

Justin:
Yes, Sensei. Start running, everyone.

Justin is a brown second white stripe belt. Kyle is a purple belt. Dyffryn is an orange belt. All of them are wearing a white karate uniform called a *dogi*; the belt is called an *obi*. Marie is taking care of the paperwork and packing it away. She waits for the warm up to finish and the students to all line up again. Justin bows to her and she bows back, showing respect to each other, not because they are family but because the student respects the instructor, what they are going to learn, and the other students. They all bow when entering the room, in thanks for a place to train. There are people who don't like or misunderstand a little about training in a church. There, they bow not just to God. They are lending their bodies to each other to be able to practise. They are trusting not to get hurt; they understand they could get hurt by accident, but not on purpose. They are giving the other person permission to practise.

Seren:
Sensei, do you speak Welsh?

Marie:
No.

Seren, one of the students, talks to her friends in Welsh while warming up. The sensei is not really paying much attention to what they are talking about, till one thing catches her attention.

Seren:
(*In Welsh*)

Fuck off.

Marie:
Seren, fifty push-ups in the corner right now. No swearing in my class.

Seren:
Sensei, you said you don't speak Welsh.

Marie:
I might choose not to speak Welsh; don't mean I don't understand it.

Seren does her fifty push-ups and knows not to speak Welsh or swear in class again, and to stick by the rules of keeping her *gi* clean and no chewing in class.

They start with the basic movements of their grades, moving up and down the hall, twenty children in the front, ten adults in the back. The adults try to avoid the children, as they take up more space. They partner up by height to practise some of the moves they have learned. They're all having fun doing takedowns. David smiles at Justin and Kyle as they try to lift their mother up. She walks around with them away from the others practising. The next thing the others see is her going backwards, hitting the floor and throwing them as they roll. She takes them forward as well. The others laugh. Dyffryn tries to join in, Justin leaves her and Kyle to grab her arms while he goes behind for a strangle hold. The sensei moves her arms to grip them, moves out and piles the three of them on each other. David takes a picture of them while laughing.

Marie does not allow bullying in her class, or outside it. The greatest strength comes from helping others and helping yourself to be a better person today than you were the day before. Don't be afraid of making mistakes, learn from them. We all fall down in life, as they do in the dojo, being taken down by their partners as they laugh and breakfall. When life throws us a curveball, some choose to stay down, some give up. In the dojo, they're given strength. When the student can get back up on their own in the dojo, when they can dust themselves down and go again, they have strength to do the same when life knocks them down. When the student that takes them down offers their hand and helps them back up, it shows them not to be afraid, but to reach out and take it. Accepting help to get back up is not weak—it shows strength, to smile and enjoy it, and to go again as they are doing right now.

People don't realise what being an instructor entails. It's not like going to school. Teachers do their part to help their students learn what they need for life, but once the students leave, the teacher's job is done and they move on to others. With martial arts, it is different; you are signing a contract for life between the both of you. Even if your students leave or even if you close the club down, even if your students have not seen you for years, even if you're old, if your students need help, they need you, and it's still your job to help. It's for life. Marie is more than a teacher.

They line back up to finish.

Marie:
What are the benefits of martial arts?

Students:
Mind, body, spirit, Sensei.

Marie:
What are the five?

Students:

MIND	BODY	SPIRIT
memory retention	balance	patience
confidence	coordination	respect
self-control	flexibility	integrity
problem-solving	muscle tone	humility
adaptation	endurance	perseverance

Marie:
Dojo Kun.

Students:

1. We will train our hearts and bodies for a firm, unshaken spirit.

2. We will pursue the true meaning of the martial way, so that in time our senses may be alert.

3. With true vigour, we will seek to cultivate a spirit of self-denial.

4. We will observe the rules of courtesy, respect our superiors and refrain from violence.

5. We will follow our religious principles and never forget the true virtue of humility.

6. We will look upwards to wisdom and strength, not seeking other desires.

7. All our lives, through the discipline of karate, we will seek to fulfil the true meaning of the Shotokan way.

They bow, making a triangle with their hands touching each other and the floor. Their nose fits in that triangle, facing the front. They first bow to the instructor, then to those behind them and to each side. They get up off their knees in grade order, seniors first after the sensei.

David:
Don't be long getting changed.

Instructors don't really charge enough for classes, if you look at what you are paying for, for yourself or your children, for £3 to £5 an hour. You're not just paying for a 'punching and kicking class'. An instructor's job is not just in class, it's outside. This is what they are:

- A life coach.
- A psychologist.
- A mentor.
- An inspirer.
- A supporter.
- A friend.
- A problem-solver.
- A stress-reliever.
- Someone who encourages you to believe in yourself.
- A personal trainer and dietician.
- Someone who teaches you personal victory.
- Someone on call for you 24/7.
- Someone who encourages you and your children to have respect, patience, humility, discipline, perseverance, empathy, courtesy, listening skills, loyalty and self-control, to name just a few things.
- Someone who teaches you how to work hard and enjoy life.
- Someone to hold you accountable for your actions.
- Someone to encourage you to set goals and to reach

your goals.

- Someone who helps you build emotional strength and mental stability.
- Someone who will hug you when you are down, pick you up when you've fallen, remind you of your worth and stand by you loyally when you feel like no one else will.
- Someone who teaches you to stand up to bullies.
- Someone who provides knowledge, wisdom, martial arts training, opportunity, training equipment and a safe dojo to train in, and who puts their heart and soul into you.
- Someone who has spent their entire life training to assist you.

Would a doctor, lawyer, plumber, carpenter, dentist, chef, mechanic, dressmaker, shop owner or psychologist offer all of the above for free in addition to the regular service that they charge for?

Marie waits for all students' parents to turn up before leaving. She is always the last to leave. While they wait, her children pull out a book from her bag to read. The book is called *Dōdō Karate Dō*. David helps take the bags to the car and drives them home.

A few weeks later, Marie has gone to Holland with her team. They are walking through the forest, watching each other's backs. They're all kitted up and armed. The wind blows through the trees and the branches sway a little, the moon shining high in the sky. They try to be as quiet as possible. They hear voices not too far away. They are there to collect intel, so they take cover in the dark and in ditches, not to be seen. Some stand behind the trees, two go up in the trees. Marie has chosen these eight, and Craig is with her. She does not speak the language, so she has chosen those who can think and translate. A mechanic and engineer, an explosives expert, driver and medic—everything a team needs. Keeping still, they listen to what is being said. When the two men stop talking, Marie gets up and starts to move out. Her team forgot she was there; she was well hidden. Seeing movement scares the two in the trees and they fall out, scaring the others as they go running. Marie gives chase after them.

They get back to headquarters and write down what they heard for her commander. Maps of the old abandoned radio station and area are pulled out. Marie and her team tried to study the ground in the morning. There's a lot of open ground to cover.

Captain Moore:
There is a mixed group of rebels from here and Germany. They are holding nine of our men along with people who worked at the place that they're being held, set up with a few Russians. They have set up a base there. Choppers will be bringing in the supplies. We think they are trying to set up for an attack under our noses. Holland asked for our help.

Craig:
Captain, you mean they don't want to lose their men. They won't miss us.

Captain Moore:
Pretty much, yes. Get it done without losing anyone. Nine captured plus thirteen other hostages. They did not attack us. NATO wants this done quietly. Staff Sergeant, you're the best I have—I'm just worried about the rest of your team that're new.

Marie:
Don't worry about them, they will be with the corporal here.

The captain looks at her, not sure what she means. She does not look at him back. Does she mean they are not going with her at all and will stay on base? Does she mean they are going, but the corporal will be in charge of them there? To him, it's riddles. Marie and Craig understand each other; he is going to have to learn the way they speak.

While Marie is away with the military, her children are missing her at home. Most homes have the mother taking care of the children, either because they're divorced, widowed or single, or because the dad spends most of his time working, but on some occasions, dads take care of their children. David happens to be one of those dads; he loves feeling useful and wanted, feeling loved by them. He misses his wife and worries when she is away. He knows when she is away, not training, she could be in danger, and he's scared that one day, there could be a knock on the door. Not to scare the children, he's told them she is away on training.

The family is sitting around the table playing Monopoly. Dyffryn is winning as she has bought Park Lane and has a hotel on it. The others are running out of money and need to sell to her. She is sitting there fidgeting with a smile on her face as they cough up the money and property.

Justin:
How do you do it? You win every time Mam's not home.

Kyle:
I think she cheats somehow. Mam wins every game when she's here. Can we play Cluedo or Ludo?

David:
Tomorrow night. Time for bed for, you three. Pack up, wash and change—I will be up to tuck you in.

David watches Dyffryn go to the front door and look up and down the street. She comes back in with her head down, closing the door behind her, then looks at her father and heads for the stairs. He watches her walk up slowly.

It is midnight, and the curtains are closed in David's room. Chinese bedding is on the bed, a way of feeling like Marie is around. Dyffryn can't sleep, and her footsteps echo across the landing as she walks from her room. There's the creak of David's bedroom door opening and closing, then Dyffryn climbs on the bed and looks at her father sleeping. She moves his arm and the blanket to get under, waking him up. He holds the blanket up for her.

David:
Can't sleep? What's wrong?

Dyffryn:
I miss Mam. When will she be home?

David smiles and nearly laughs at the thought.

David:
You, missing Mam? Thought you were a daddy's girl. I miss her too, so do your brothers.

Dyffryn:
I know, and I am a daddy's girl, but I miss Mam. I love her too.

David:
It's no good telling me that you love her when she has gone away, she needs to hear it from you from time to time. I know you love us; Mam does know you love her. She loves you very much.

Dyffryn:
I know. Why does she have to be away so long? It's been three weeks now.

David:
Her job is very important to others; people's lives depend on her. She must get her team trained. She will be home before you know it.

Dyffryn:
Can I sleep in here tonight please, Dad?

David:
Just tonight, then back in your room. Now go to sleep, you've got school.

In Holland, Marie takes her team out to the field on a rescue mission. No vehicle drops—she doesn't want the sound of engines approaching. Walking through the streets, it's like a ghost town, dust and debris everywhere. There is no way they can get close enough to the building without being seen and getting the hostages killed. Marie places her men to surround the building and wait till dark for cover, taking time to blend in to stay hidden the best they can. She walks off in a different direction on her own, leaving them there to watch and wait for orders. It's quiet, just the feel of the wind on their faces, the moon in the sky.

A few hours have gone by, and Marie has made it inside the building alone, working her way up the floors, trying to be as quiet as possible. People are walking around, armed to their teeth. Marie uses an endoscope to look round corners, as she is very close to the floor where the hostages are being held. Getting to them is one thing, getting them out safe is another.

A door opens, and two men walk out together, heading down the corridor past her. She catches the door with her foot at the last second and waits. When it is safe, she opens the door a little bit, and looks inside. The hostages are in the corner of the room, hands on their heads. One man has been shot in the leg and sits there with a coat wrapped around it.

Her team outside are getting nervous out in the open. The waiting and not knowing is making their hearts race quicker the longer they are there. It's been hours; daylight will be approaching soon. They'd feel better if they knew what was happening. Why are they not moving inside? They're thinking, *What is the staff sergeant waiting for*, not realising she has gone in alone. They watch their surroundings and the windows.

Inside, the room starts to fill with gas from the canisters Marie has rolled towards the men sitting at the radios. She puts on a gas mask, and gunshots sound as men fall to the floor from being shot in the legs. They're firing in all directions, expecting a team of soldiers entering—the staff sergeant had thrown a Thunderflash to give that illusion. The gunshots give their positions away, and she shoots them dead where they stand.

Her men hear the gunshots outside. Craig knows she has gone in alone with no backup.

The nine soldiers being held as hostages are badly beaten but can move. She links their hands together like a chain to walk them out of the room. She picks up the wounded man and carries him on her shoulders. They make their way out of the building. The men left inside start shooting from windows; her team starts firing back to give them cover. She leads the rescued hostages in a line, each holding the one in front of them, keeping the civilians between them. A chopper flies overhead to land in the distance, and she sends her men to capture it. The pilot is not needed as she has her own.

She waits for her team to come back, then they leave with the hostages. There is the sound of a huge bang, and a cloud of dust rises over the land and into the sky as they fly over in the chopper. The others have no idea what has happened, but see the building is now gone as the dust and rubble start to settle. Marie's team start to treat the wounded in the chopper on the way back. All have questions about what really happened.

Marie and her team return to Crickhowell in the evening. Everyone that is not on guard is in the NAAFI drinking and eating pizza when the team gets off the truck with their gear. They join the others. Everyone is excited to see them return and hugs them, handing drinks to them. They take a seat, and pizza arrives in front of them. Four hours fly by, and at 23:00 hours, as the NAAFI closes, they head for bed. The men sleep in the buildings; the women have got the old air raid shelters.

In the early hours of the morning, 2 a.m., Marie is awake. The door opens as the light goes on—inspection time. A surprise for the army cadets staying there. The children are not happy about being woken up, all in pyjamas as they stand by their beds half asleep. Their lockers are checked to make sure that they have everything in the correct order, which can't be done if the cadets have their uniforms on. They leave, and the girls get ready for the day, wearing their lightweight uniform. They iron their creases, some polish their boots. Once they're done, they all line up outside, ready for the day ahead, a treat for them. This only comes around once in a lifetime—not every cadet will get to do it.

The cadets make their way and stand together in lines. There is a bed outside with an officer sleeping in his pants. Everyone is looking at him. The regimental sergeant major (RMS) is standing on the balcony, and sends men down to shift the officer and the bed. Corporal Craig wakes up to find himself in the middle of what is going on, covers himself with the blanket and walks in to get dressed, looking at his staff sergeant, knowing they are in trouble. While the cadets wait for the UN trucks to arrive to take them, a thirteen-year-old boy decides to ask his sergeant a question, making Marie smile, trying not to laugh. The others in line can't help themselves.

Rhys:
Sarge, can we have a fag while we wait?

The sergeant was not happy about the question asked: smoking underage.

Sergeant Morrison:
Son, you smoke when I smoke.

Rhys:
But Sarge, you don't smoke.

Everyone starts to laugh. Trucks arrive, and they get on at 4 a.m.

They arrive in London Buckingham Palace for Trooping the Colour. The cadets are in uniform—no denim allowed, smart dress only—and they take their seats in the stands with others. David Beckham and a few other celebrities sit there. It's a nice sunny day, and people are waving British flags. Grenadier Company comes first. Following behind them are the Right Flank Coldstream Company; following behind them are the Left Flank Scots Company. There is no lead company for the Irish; they have a mascot, an Irish wolfhound. Fifth is the Prince of Wales Company. The whole Household Division is marching, made up of five foot regiments and two cavalry regiments, blue and royals and lifeguards. The Welsh Guards are there, smart in their £500 bearskins. Their tunics are a thousand pounds each, not counting the rest of the uniform and equipment. The officers wear different coloured bands with their regiment badges. Grenadier, red band. Coldstream, white band. Scots guards, tartan band. Irish, green band. Welsh, black and green with the leek badge. The guards adopted the bearskin after winning the Battle of Waterloo. The band is playing, the Queen waving to the crowd from her horse-drawn carriage. When it ends, the cadets all line up outside and are counted, waiting for the trucks to arrive and pick them all up again.

After that, they go to the Sennybridge Mountains and training area. The cadets of England and Wales wake up in their tents on the tree-covered mountainside where the grass is so green. They get dressed into uniform, sort out their sleeping bags, pack down the tents, sort out breakfast for themselves and top up their canteens full of water. When they're all packed up to go, the smallest and slowest walk in front as the others follow in line behind, carrying their kit and gun, following a map given to them so they can read the grid reference. They drink their water as they cross over the mountaintops, and eventually they come to a stream to make tea and food. They clean up their mess tins in the stream water as they pack up, and top their canteens back up from the stream, dropping a white tablet in to kill any germs that could make them ill.

They start walking again. The bags on their backs weigh a lot, but they manage well with stops for breaks. They reach a windy mountaintop with a cliff drop on one side. A small young girl, thirteen years old, struggles to walk across the top. You would think the weight of the bag would be heavy enough to hold her, but instead, the wind catches the bag and blows it to the side, taking her with it. Marie and Sergeant Malcolm Morrison send Justin Hunter and another cadet to the girl's side to hold her between them and stop her being blown away. The sergeant carries her bag on top of his till they get off the top.

They get to safety and stagger their lines with the last cadets walking backwards, watching their backs for them. They stop in an open field, and the two large platoons make a circle lying on the floor, England on the right and Wales on the left. They face out with guns pointing out, one foot under and the other over the feet of the people either side of them, a way to know where their teammates are and that they're distanced correctly. Justin is working out where to go on the map when he sees a girl from the England side get up and run into the tree line behind him. Justin looks up to what has caught his attention, flying overhead in the sky.

Justin:
No one move! Keep very still.

Everyone starts to get nervous, not knowing what is going on, expecting a loud bang from a grenade or a mine. Marie moves in slowly and grabs the snake by its tail—good job it's not a venomous snake, but a constrictor. Both officers carefully move the snake away from the cadets and let it go on its way. Why did the girl have to throw the snake in their direction, why could she not have thrown it the other way? They slowly collect themselves after what just happened, then start to move out in two teams. If one gets caught by the enemy, the other can finish the mission or be their backup or both. It is not a competition between them; this is life training and experience for if they wish to join up at eighteen.

The cadets take cover in ditches and behind trees as they follow their map to an empty building. It is getting dark and they need somewhere to sleep. Tents would give them away, so the officers go inside as the cadets give cover. Inside, there are two huge fans and concrete steps leading up a few levels, large enough that they can fit two people sleeping side by side with a gap between them. The cadets move in one by one. The fans are off, thank God. They pull out their sleeping bags and put them on the cold concrete floor before getting in fully clothed, boots on, gun beside them. The two officers stay awake on watch outside in the night. The sky is pitch black; they can't see anything. That's dangerous, no stars in the sky. Some of the cadets struggle to sleep from the cold. The cadets are afraid at the thought of the noise and cold from the two huge fans if they were to start up again.

At 4 a.m., Marie walks in with a torch, finds her son, Justin, and has him pack up and walk out with no torch in the pitch black to scout without a party, telling him to stay covered. At 5 a.m., she does the same with the English party. The sergeant was worried about them heading out in the darkness alone; they could get killed by the wildlife or the land, anything could happen to them.

At 6 a.m., when it starts to get light, the officers wake the rest of the cadets up and wait for them to pack up. They hand two maps to two new leaders to get them to where they need to be. The others are wondering where the original team leaders have got to—what time did they leave? But still they walk through streams, climb mountains and rocks, helping each other as a team should do.

Marie:
Right, you spread out and signal to each other. Find your team leaders, they are hiding here somewhere. They have information you need, if they have done their jobs in the morning. Go.

When he left camp, Justin took out a knife he carries with him—after all, they are trained to never go anywhere without a knife. A knife is a tool and not a weapon; even if it can kill people, it's a tool with a purpose, as they say. Justin made marks on trees so he could find his way back, but no one else would be able to follow him because the marks blend in on the tree trunks. He gets to the border of the training area and sees movement. As he climbs a tree and marks it, he makes a mental note of what he can see. He sees an English cadet turn up an hour later and drops his knife by the boy's feet. The cadet stops and looks up, and Justin gives a signal to climb. The cadet climbs up with his knife and returns it to him, then they mark down everything they need to remember together. As it starts to get light, they both climb down and follow the markings back until they hear a sound. They take cover in ditches not to be seen. It's just deer, but they do not know this, so they keep quiet and do not move. The cadets close their positions and find the English cadet amongst tree branches and leaves, because the cadet started moving them so he could see the others. Justin on the other hand, they can't find him at all.

Once two hours have gone by, Marie knows they are not going to find him. The sergeant is worried that he is lost. Marie tells the cadets to all stay where they are till she gets back, and then she follows the marks left on the trees. She stops and looks to the ground, seeing insects moving around. She follows them slowly. Well-hidden, out of the way, she comes across a nest of different creatures. She has found her son.

Marie:
Cadet, you're safe now. Let's join the others.

Justin:
How did you know where I was, ma'am? The others all walked past me.

Marie:
Mother Nature gave you away. I bet those bugs have been eating you alive. Let's get you sorted. Well done, by the way. You will need to get changed, use your sleeping bag. Between you and I, I did exactly the same as you as a cadet. No one found me, I was covered in insects in the night, I did not move to check the time, I did not know they had stopped looking for me—in fact, they had forgotten about me. They all got back to NAAFI and only realised it at the end of NAAFI at 23:00 hours. I worked my way back to find the others eating and drinking.

Recently, when I was trying to learn information from the enemy, I hid in a ditch with the others. Two of my team were in trees. When I moved and started running, my team forgot I was there again, curled up in the dark in a corner beside them. I scared the crap out of them! The two in the trees fell out and landed on their bums.

I had a feeling with you, that you might have done the same, so I looked for insects. Nature is a good giveaway.

Justin:
You're going to tell the others.

Marie:
No, I won't say a thing, it's our secret. As your mother, I am very proud of you. I love you.

Justin:
As your son, are you trying to ask me something? Like, am I here to be with you, or to be like you, or am I doing this for myself? You don't have to worry there. This is all me, because I want to do this for myself. It was a nice surprise when you turned up at Crickhowell. This is a great week away. I think you are volunteering to be here to do this to spend time with us instead of going home. I'm not sure if it is to spend time with me or if you're supporting all the cadets?

Marie:
It's both, this time around. I always do this if I get back on time before going home. This time, you're here too, so we'll go home together. I'll walk in after you to surprise them, ok?

They get back to the others. Justin gets cream for his bites and takes his kit to change; his mates help get the insects off and out of his kit. Once he's changed, he takes his canteen and his mother's, wets the ground to make mud, then takes his knife and starts to draw what he saw with the help of the other cadet. They have rescue officers in the buildings Justin scouted.

They all move out in formation, using the ditches and tunnels, taking out men by sneaking up on them. The enemy knows if they are caught, they should play dead, as if this was real, they would have possibly died. It would be wrong to do this with real fighting, beating children up. They are there to learn and have fun. The children get caught and some of them play dead. Sneaking around, trying not to make a noise, struggling to look around corners and move out without getting caught, Justin holds his team back behind him. He tries to use his knife edge to look for movement, or a shadow on the floor.

The buildings, old air raid shelters, are very dirty and full of stones from outside that have got in. As the cadets block the doors and tap the roof, the people inside try to get out, so the children get on top. The blockage of the door is moved, three guys jump out and the children jump them. The children work their way around the place. A few smoke bombs go off and a group of children race to the officers that are hostages and start to move out of the room. As they get outside, Justin sets off a flare to say the enemies are dead and the hostages rescued. When a second flare goes up in a different colour, Craig and his men pop up from everywhere, surrounding them and shooting them all with paint guns. Justin looks at his mother and the sergeant. Marie smiles at them all.

Marie:
Well done, cadets. I really mean that, you did well. We couldn't help but join in with you! The lesson here is there can always be a traitor in your squad. Whether it is a rank below you, or above you. Sometimes you have to take your own officers out. Don't be afraid to do things alone. I sent the two of you in alone—less is sometimes more. Keep the others for backup and as support to get you out—don't keep them all in the middle of things, or you might lose everyone. Ok, let's get back.

The following day is games: rugby and football for the boys, hockey for the girls. As cadets sometimes get hurt, the military medics stay busy patching up injuries with plasters or bandages as needed. People try to cheat by hitting each other, hockey sticks to kneecaps. Children will be children. Trophies are given to the winners to take home with them.

After the long day, everyone is back at their dorms. The boys get a nice clean building with beds and lockers; the girls are in a horrible air raid shelter, with mushrooms growing in the corners, flying beetles, spiders and slugs which get into boots. There's one door with a light switch by it. The beds go all the way up both sides and across the back, and there are lockers in the middle, back-to-back up the centre. When the door is closed and the lights are out, it is pitch black. You can't see anything at all—you have to shout to the sergeant for the light if you wish to move and go to the toilet. You make sure you hide in your sleeping bag well so you won't be bitten by insects at night.

Everyone is fast asleep at midnight when one of the cadets decides not to wake the sergeant up, thinking she could work her way from the top of the air raid shelter to get to the door to go to the toilet. Everyone is woken up by two thuds—the first one metal, the second the floor. The sergeant, Sarah McGrath, is an ambulance driver in real life, when not looking after the cadets. She starts treating the child who knocked herself out by walking into the lockers.

The next morning is the adults' games. Marie is a back right defender in hockey. The men's games were cancelled after the stunt they played with Craig and disciplinary for behaviour. The hockey starts, and Marie is taking some hits. They lose the game.

Marie has to have her knee checked. The second game begins, and they keep it equal as they play, point to point, never cheating, a good game. They draw at the end, putting Marie's team through for the last game. Marie's team plays well without having to cheat, and wins the game.

When the fun starts for them is England vs Wales. Dragon vs Lions. War begins. There is no way in hell the English are going to beat the Welsh on their own turf. England tries to cheat and take out knees and ankles, and the Welsh have to use their reserves. Wales do not drop to their way of playing and do not cheat. It makes the English angry as the points get away from them. Wales win. Holding the trophy, they're each given medals to take home. People are limping, but there's no hard feelings—they are all friends after it. Friendly games just get out of hand.

Everyone gets packed and changed to go home by the end of the day. Marie looks at the picture of her family waiting for her back at home. She has been away for a month.

When she gets home, she walks in with a limp and cuts on her legs as the children run to hug her. David hugs and kisses her, looks at her and shakes his head. He takes her stuff from her and carries it in. He runs a hot bath for her with bubbles and scented candles. Marie lies in there and soaks. David brings her a cup of tea and sits on the side of the bath.

David:
Are you feeling better now? The kids missed you. I enjoyed your time away and did not miss you at all.

Marie:
Liar. I missed you all too.

David:
I was thinking, if you're not working tomorrow, I can drop the kids with their granddad, we can spend the night together relaxing, I can take the day off, William can take them to school and pick them up. We can relax together. We can order Chinese and a glass of wine or more.

Marie:
Sounds good to me. So nice to be home.

Marie puts her tea on the side. David leans in for a kiss, Marie can't help herself; she pulls him in with her. She has a big smile on her face, laughing inside. They hold each other, kissing. David moves, dripping wet, pushes her head underwater, messing around. He lets her go straight away.

Takes a towel, wipes her face for her, hands her tea back to finish. He leaves to get changed and takes the kids to pop to the shops.

David looks around the shop, picking up flowers, Ferrero Rocher chocolates and a couple of bottles of wine. He decides to cook her dinner, picks up candles. He'll make the curry fresh. He gets everything he needs, pays and leaves.

Back home, David walks in to find his wife lying on the settee with just a towel wrapped around her. He puts the shopping in the kitchen and joins her with a smile on his face. He sits by her feet and takes them in his hands and starts to massage. She smiles with her eyes closed. He slowly starts to move his hand up her leg and back a little bit at a time, further each time, as if teasing under the towel. She takes his hands when he gets too close and pulls him towards her for kisses. He lies on top of her, holding her.

Marie:
Still love me then?

David:
No, I just love your body. Course I still love you. Do you still love me? Not wanting to trade for a younger model? Hope I still please you sexually. I know your seven sexual points, every part of your body, what triggers your sexual points.

Marie:
You like your ear nibbled on, kisses on the neck, back and foot massage, a blow job, then love-making.

David:
You love to be fingered, eaten, then hours of sex to follow. I am fancying dessert right now. Stay like that—we are going straight to bed. Or we can have fun here right now.

Marie:
I am going to trade you in for a slightly younger model, and watch *The Greatest Showman*, and have a glass of wine. You can join us.

David:
Spoilsport. Dinner first, I'll get something on. If you had your way, this would be all or nothing at all. That can come later. Ok, don't put too much on—no need for clothes really, just us. Put your short blue thin silk nighty on, so I can see your arse and get my hands on you. Put on your blue silk dolphin dressing gown. I will keep you warm.

Marie:
Let me up. Come on, let me up. You are not going to get anything if you don't let me up. I will be right back, love.

Later, David and Marie are sitting in their nightwear watching the film and drinking together on the settee, cuddled together enjoying each other's company. David tries to distract her joking by nibbling her ears, running his fingers up and down her back, up and down her legs, keeping her warm. Getting her in the mood, ready for bed.

A few weeks later, the three children go running into their parents' room like normal. But this time, instead of waking them up on a Saturday morning, they've decided to do something different. David and Marie are facing each other, cuddling and asleep. Dyffryn climbs on the bed onto her father's back and side, waking up her mother. Marie helps her by turning David more for her to lie on his back. Kyle decides to do the same on his mother's back. Justin can lie on the bed next to her as she holds his arm over them all to cuddle in together. All under the blankets, they sleep for an extra hour. David wakes up and realises they are all in bed together. He watches everyone sleep, not used to the children not jumping on them. It feels odd. He lies there, thinking about what to do for the day.

David:
(*Whispering*)

Marie, Marie. Morning. How about we take them to the beach today, on the rides?

Marie:
It's going to be a nice day—why not? What time is it?

David:
We did sleep in, it's 10 a.m. It's not like the boys. We'll give them an hour and then we'll make a move.

Justin:
I'm awake. I've got a bad feeling. My guts hurt. Can we stay home this weekend please? I feel sick.

David:
That's not like you. Fresh air will do you some good. Think of these two.

Marie:
I'll stay here with him. You take these two and have a good day together.

They all go in the end. They arrive at Porthcawl Beach. The sun is in the sky, and there's the noise of the rides as the music plays and the crowd of people enjoy themselves, eating candy floss, doughnuts and ice cream. People are sitting outside the pubs drinking, buying lunch at the fast takeaways, sitting in the café or at high tide. Children are on the rides as they go round and in the arcades. Marie hates the sand, and the beach is full of people building sandcastles, kicking footballs around, flying kites, throwing Frisbees or swimming in the sea. Marie stands at the wall at the top of the steps to watch. David sorts the children out first then goes back for Marie and throws her over his shoulder. She grips on for dear life. She thought she could get away with just watching them from the glass barriers. Justin takes off her shoes and socks and puts them on the rock. David puts her down on the sand. She feels the hot sand between her toes.

David and Marie bury the children and make sand statues with them. Dyffryn is a mermaid. The boys together are a sea monster. The children work together to bury their mother and father. David is the devil. Marie is an angel. Marie can't wait to get out and have a shower. The children take photos of them. After that, they head for the car for a change of clothes. They get changed at a pub and sit down for a drink. They all have soft drinks. Marie knows she still has sand on her and hates it. She can't wait to get home for a bath, but she does not want to ruin the day for the children. She keeps watching Justin, knowing he is not feeling well. She has the same feeling as her son, but she says nothing. She wants them all close to her.

Marie heads for the toilet, and the children are curious about their mother.

Justin:
Dad, why does Mam hate the sand so much? Not just the sand, but pool water too?

David:
Ask your mother. Here she comes.

Marie:
When you get older, there are things you once enjoyed but you no longer do. I hate the sand stuck to my feet, it gets everywhere in the car and at home, and I hate having to clean it off. I don't like the smell of chlorine; it makes me feel sick, so I avoid it as much as possible. Just ask your father, he will know. Yes, you buried me today. Does not mean I enjoyed it. I just enjoyed watching you have fun doing it. All I really want right now is a bath and my pyjamas.

David:
Hey, you cheeky cow. Yes, things do change, but not just because you're old.

Dyffryn:
Dad, don't you mean 'you're ancient'? You're way past old!

Marie starts laughing and so do the others. David looks at Marie, as he knows that this is all her doing. She can't look back at him. They get up and head for the rides. They stand in the queue with others.

David:
I think it's my turn to crush Dyffryn. Then bowling, pool and a drink, I think. We all have chosen something. Ice cream after the rides. As the saying goes: I scream, you scream, we all scream for ice cream!

David likes teasing his children. They're queuing for a ride that goes round and forces the people on the inside to crush the people on the outside. Marie says nothing and tries not to laugh, but she has a smile on her face. Dyffryn panics a little in case David is being serious.

Dyffryn:
You can't crush me, Dad.

David:
Why not? It's my turn after all

Dyffryn:
Mam, tell him he can't crush me.

Dyffryn looks at her mother for help and hides behind her, holding her hand for support. They're waiting for the ride to stop so they can get on.

David:
I see. Calling Mam in for help and backup. The women are

going to gang up on me now. I remember that. So much for being a daddy's girl.

Marie:
David, you can't crush her. Kyle will be in the middle of Dad and Dyffryn. Help her crush your father. Justin and I will sit in the one behind you.

Dyffryn moves from her mother, holds her brother's hand and waits by the ride, which has finally come to a stop and people are getting off. The ride owner moves the rope for people to get on, taking the tickets from them. Dyffryn choses the seat she wants. David picks her up and helps her in, then does the same for Kyle before getting in himself. Justin waits next to them before going on himself.

Justin:
Dad, you should know by now you will not win in this family.

David:
You two traitors. You were supposed to side with me. Men against the women, out-voted. I see where I stand now.

Dyffryn enjoys crushing her brother and father, then the three children go to the ghost train to scare themselves. David and Marie know they will be fine together; Justin will take good care of his brother and sister. They are giving their parents time together to go on a ride at the same time. Dyffryn is too small to go on the beach party ride anyway. The beach party doesn't just go up as it swings back and forth, it circles around, and they love the view as they twist on it and go upside down.

As they come to a stop, they see a metal cage has come off one of the rides with a child inside. People run to help from all directions. Marie runs ahead, but David and the children slowly walk over. They are scared of what they are about to see, thinking the worst. Security runs to the area to keep people back, people try to call emergency services, the child's parents are frantic. Marie and David start pushing people out of the way. Marie gets in the cage and finds the child has a broken arm and leg and is slowly dying from internal damage as a broken rib has punctured his lung. Kyle watches from a distance. Marie has a bottle of water with her, and she tips a little water over both her hands, then over the boy's head and chest.

Marie closes her eyes and drops her head to the boy's ear. She whispers to him something that no one else can hear. Kyle notices a little light between his mother's hand and the boy. Stunned and not knowing what to make of what is happening, he starts to think that his mother might be a witch—but how can that be possible? There is no such thing as witches. Are the stories from the past actually true? He's afraid to say anything to his brother and sister; they might think he has gone crazy from the sight. Fixated on his mother and the boy, he's unable to turn his head and look away.

Everyone's hearts are racing and they're all worried. Paramedics are pushing through the crowd. As they get close to the cage, Marie stands up and helps the boy to his feet as if nothing has happened.

Marie:
David, help me get him out please. He is fine to move.
Careful, that's it.

After that, they shut the fair down due to the accident. The paramedics check the boy over at the ambulance with the parents standing there. The boy is fine and everyone is surprised that there is not a mark on him or anything wrong with him. Marie takes her kids' hands and walks to the bowling place to settle after what just happened. They play bowling and pool, trying to beat each other, and have a few drinks. They're trying to get over the shock of what has happened and take the children's minds off it all. Kyle can't help but keep looking over to his mother from time to time, looking at her hands.

Marie:
I have something you can try and beat each other at. You need two pool cues and a ball. You have to try and get that ball from the bottom of the cue to the top without touching it or dropping it.

Kyle:
There's no way that can be done. Balls don't run up hills, only down them. We're not stupid, you know. Can't fool us with that.

Marie:
Yes, it can. Just work it out.

They all try, but keep dropping the ball on the table. Even David can't do it. All five take it in turns. Marie manages it every time. David gets it. The children struggle but eventually do it, and there are smiles on their faces when they finally succeed. They had a crowd starting to watch what they were trying to do, fascinated by it. When they leave the table, the crowd gathered have to try it as well. The family grab their things and leave for the car.

They are in the car on the way home. It is late and dark. David notices they are being followed for some time by cars and four-by-fours. He moves his left hand onto Marie's leg and squeezes a little a couple of times to get her attention. Marie looks at his hand then back at him. He's trying not to scare the children. He moves his hand off her leg and points to the mirror. He adjusts the left mirror for her to see the car following them then adjusts it back. They are a few streets away from home. When a car pulls out in front of them, making them slow down and stop, David decides to reverse back up the street as the car in front is coming at him. The car behind does not move. David can see a side street to turn in. As he gets to it, a car comes across from another side street and rams right into the side of him. The children are scared and crying. People with guns get out of the four vehicles and slowly start walking towards them.

Marie:
Justin, take your coat off now. Grab my jacket and Dad's. Cover yourselves and get low. Whatever happens, you do not move or make a sound. Now get behind the car seats.

David:
It's James. Marie, get your head down.

Marie moves her hand to her necklace and starts playing with it. David covers her body with his as he lies across her. Marie quietly talks to herself, not for others to hear her. David reaches his left hand towards the children through the gap in the seats. The boys with guns start shooting at the car, hitting body work and the glass. There are the sounds of bullets hitting metal. Glass shatters all over them. The men come over to the car, and the children stay hidden until they leave.

It all goes quiet after the cars race off. Justin moves very slowly and can see blood has sprayed all over the inside of the car. Blood runs over the children, from the parents lying there. In the car, a bright light had shone on the children, just barely touching the parents. They think it must have been a streetlight giving off that much light. But there's no lamppost there. None of them really notice it, except for Kyle, who's looking at his mother's hand, which is glowing with a little blue light again. The children do not know if their parents are alive or dead. Dyffryn is screaming. Justin lifts his head to check his parents; he finds a piece of glass and uses it to see outside. No one is around. He moves and gets his brother and sister out of the car as safely as he can.

Justin:

You two, help me get Mam out of the car. Come on, pull. I'll lift Dad, you pull. Lay her down. Now help me with Dad.

The children are wiping their eyes, but still tears run down their faces. They struggle to move their parents, not sure they should be moving them at all. Justin knows that his father is putting pressure on his mother's wounds by lying on her, but his father needs help and they can't help in that position. They are children and panicking to save their parents. The blood that covers their hands makes it harder to hold, so they grab the clothing at first. Using martial arts training to lift together helps.

Kyle:
He's heavy.

Justin:
Dead weight. Hold on. Dyffryn, you can help get his legs out. I will go around to the passenger's side and push him up. Kyle, you hold him. Give me a second. Ok, pushing, hold him there. I'm coming back to help you. Ok, Dyffryn, get his legs out first. Kyle, help me pull him and lay him down. Pull now.

Kyle:
What do we do now? Are they still alive?

Dyffryn:
I want Mammy and Daddy. Get up. Please wake up. Make them wake up.

Justin:
Grab a mobile phone from the car. Phone 999 and ask for an ambulance. You two cover Mam and apply pressure to stop the bleeding. I will do the same with Dad.

People start running to help the children. Kyle moves his parents' hands to each other as if to let them hold hands again. Justin just looks at him in confusion, but thinks it's a nice gesture. Kyle can't see the blue light on his mother's hands and his heart is sinking fast. Other people take over as the police and ambulance turn up and start treating the parents. Police close the road off. Blue lights are flashing everywhere, police are putting up barriers and tape all over the place, keeping people back from the crime scene. They're trying to take statements from any witnesses around. Paramedics help the children off their parents to treat them. The two boys go in the ambulance with their father. Dyffryn is with her mother.

The blue sky turns grey as the light fades, clouds gather and it starts to rain. The children notice in the ambulances that their parents' wedding rings and necklace are missing. The men didn't just shoot them, but robbed them. The police found no purse or wallets in the car. The children get treated for shock. The police are looking at the car and see bullet holes through the seats and the coats that covered the children. They look back at the paramedics and the children, wondering how the children got away without a graze or bullet in them. How did they survive?

Months later, Justin and the children go back to school. Justin has tried to focus on everything he could do for his brother and sister. It is what their parents would have wanted him to do. Living with their granddad has not been easy; they miss their parents so much.

Dyffryn is in class. The afternoon's lesson is about the planet.

Dyffryn:
Miss, if the planet is moving around in a circle, and the moon and sun circle around us too, why don't we get dizzy and fly off the Earth?

Mrs Taltson:
Good question. Gravity is what holds us to the planet. You cannot see it, but you can feel it. Your body feels heavy.

What stops the Earth from spinning too fast and sending us off course is our Mother Nature. Deadly as it can be, it is what saves us at the same time.

Dyffryn:
Miss, I don't understand. How can something that kills us, save us?

The teacher is drawing on the blackboard, explaining what is happening for the children to see.

Mrs Taltson:
Look at the four elements: fire, earth, water, air. These slow the planet down from spinning so fast. Let's start with air. Places like America get tornadoes spinning so fast that they destroy everything in their path. Terrifying as it is for people—yes, people die, homes get destroyed—it works against the planet in a way that it slows us down. It's like if you walked backwards into a crowd of people, eventually the crowd would slow you down or stop you.

Take earth. The earthquakes we get underground make holes appear in the roads and the earth shake, making everything fall and collapse on things. The core stones move and collide with each other and help slow the planet down.

Now look at fire and water. They both have something in common.

Fire first—it burns all the trees and grass. Fire destroys and kills, yes, but the animals need it to survive. Where there is no more grass and only weeds and things that animals can't eat, the fire destroys it. New growth starts, giving animals food to eat. Then we have the lava that comes from volcanoes, causing everything to burn. It is like water; it runs down mountains and across land. Eruptions and lava falling into the seas slow it down.

Water feeds the land, us, animals, plant life. It can also take life away by drowning us. Look at the storms and tides: waves hit rock and crash onto our lands. The tides and waves crashing are what pulls against our planet and slows us down.

Everything has a design and purpose in life. Trees give us oxygen to breathe. They soak up a lot of water. If we get rid of all those trees off the mountain, we'll have nothing to hold the water back and it will flood our homes. Just like all creatures big and small: without them, we will die. We need plants and food, and the animals all take care of plants or deal with dung, like beetles. They rely on all the elements to survive. We take care of Mother Nature's creatures; Mother Nature takes care of us.

Kyle is in class learning about the Rhondda, Welsh words and their meanings. He tries to write it all down. Kyle has always liked the Welsh names of places where his friends live. He's proud to be Welsh. As the saying goes, you can take a person out of Wales, but you can't take Wales out of the person. The teacher writes down all the names of the places on the blackboard as she explains them.

Justin's school trip has come around. His parents had bought him a new bag for it, and books, pens, etc. As he looks at them and remembers his parents, he is in a world of his own for a few minutes till he snaps out of it. He checks he has everything he needs, and the new wallet his father had bought him. He empties his bag and checks it all again. Others watch him do it, and he does not realise they are there.

His teachers and classmates are not sure whether to say something to him or not. They have no idea what he is going through or how he feels—how will he react if they ask? The tension between them and him, you can cut with a knife. Justin finds it hard to be with his classmates, without seeing his father at school and riding in with him and back home. He's slowly withdrawn into himself, away from his friends, as he's lost interest in life. Right now, he's just focused on his studies and his family. It is what his parents would have wanted, and he doesn't want to let them down at all.

He trails behind his class on the trip, keeping his space. He looks at the forest as birds fly above him, free to come and go as they like. A simple life—as the saying goes, free as a bird. They just have to learn to fly, make nests and mate, simple things. Food and water are easy to find all around. With humans, it's just greed.

While the children are at school, William Thomas is walking across Porthcawl Beach, water hitting his ankles, deep in thought, full of sorrow. The smell of the sea is on the breeze blowing against his skin. There are clouds in the blue sky, and an urn in his hand. Children are in the water, others play on the beach. Joggers run past listening to music. He walks to the seafront steps as waves lap against them, then opens the urn and pours some of the ashes into his hand. The wind takes a little.

William:
I kept my word, I just don't want to let you go. I thought keeping you with me would mean you are still with me, that doing this would be losing you forever, my love. Now I feel like I'm freeing you. You're not bound to the house, but free to move with me everywhere. I feel that you are with me still. The children are living with me now. I find it hard sometimes, and what to say to them... you were the one with words. How do I say to them that everything will be fine when they are not? I don't know how much longer I have myself—where does that leave them? I need you now, more than ever.

William pours the ashes into the sea and sits down with his eyes closed. He slowly dozes off, but a voice from the wind and sea wakes him up. He stands and sees the person calling him.

Lillian:
Bill, Bill, wake up, my love. It is me. I love you too. We will be together again, but not any time soon. Please don't say anything—I have a short time, so please listen. The children will be fine. They have you, Lucy and Kieran to help them right now; they are not alone in any way.

Danger lies ahead. You must keep your heads, family must hold strong together. We have forgotten who we are. Remember. Now you need to wake up. The tide is in and you are about to drown. Wake up, my love, wake up.

William wakes up and a wave pushes him, moving him off the step. The urn is taken by the sea. He gets to his feet and moves up on the front, away from the water. He stands looking out to the sea, catching a glimpse of his wife as she fades away for the last time. His daughter is by her side. He rubs his eyes, and there's nothing. He is just dreaming. He is tired, wet and cold. He walks back to his car.

Later, William is at home and the children are home from school, helping with the cleaning, when a song comes on the radio: Queen, 'I Want to Break Free'. William and Justin laugh with the duster and polish and hoover, pretending to dance like Queen, lightening the mood a little.

Dyffryn:
Granddad, I don't understand why Mam and Dad got shot? Why didn't we? The police were whispering in the hospital. When will they catch them?

William:
I have no idea why our family was targeted or why you three got lucky. I am grateful for it, I could not lose you all. I thank God for it.

Justin:
I do, I know why. It's all my fault. I couldn't save us.

William:
It's not your fault, and it's not your job to protect us. You did save your brother and sister, yourself too. You listened to your mother and father, and Marie did what she had to. Your mother and father saved you. It's how it is supposed to be. They would be proud of you all.

Kyle:
I know why we weren't hurt—it was magic. I just don't understand why they got shot? I miss them both.

Justin:
No such thing as magic, just tricks.

William:
Your mother got her sense of humour from my brother and myself. My brother and I were in Germany, your mother was there. She would laugh her head off at us. Before she met your father, we were in a military base in Berlin. Every time a guard said he was from Three Company, my brother and your mother would get away with murder. She would say 'Metal Mickey little iron men'. Then we called Two Company 'Blockheads'. For Prince of Wales—we could not say POW. It was not insulting enough, so, 'piss of wind'. When I fought for the Welsh Guards, my brother, being much younger than me, he was a corporal, he went over to the Falklands War. He was on a boat, nearly in enemy territory, and he accidentally dropped his gun overboard when it should have been strapped to him. His sergeant, he was with the Blockheads, made him carry a 48 all over the land—he was given a second gun. His sergeant made him know he'd fucked up. It went all around the military. The guy is still alive today to tell the story. There are so many stories; it's just so hard to talk about the war. Civvies just won't understand at all. I know you're a cadet, but that's different. That's nothing.

Justin:
Yeah, well Mam never made it feel like nothing, but a start of something. She made it feel special. She was proud of us, proud of me doing it. She even took time out for me. Not just me, for my friends and others—she went to support them and offered her time. That is special. She never made us feel worthless, even when we messed up. She never looked down on us. Just because you're still with the military...

William:
Only things I love in life and am loyal to are me, my Queen and my regiment. No one or nothing is before them.

Justin:
Let's get out of here. We don't need him, I can take care of us. We are going home, not staying here.

Kyle:
I don't think he means it; I think he is just hurting right now. Look, the urn has gone.

Dyffryn:
Please, Justin, can we stay tonight? He needs us—he is missing Mum and Gran. Please? Granddad, we'll finish cleaning, go get some sleep.

William:
Sorry, kids, I think it is time for you all to start spending time with your friends again. You can't stay cooped up inside, it is not healthy for you. Can't count school. Start doing things from tomorrow. I do love you all. Been a bad day for me.

Dyffryn:
I miss our pool and home.

Kyle:
Maybe we can just go back tomorrow. I just want to swim in our pool again, Granddad, please. I miss my room.

William:
Yes, you're right, everything you need is there. I will pack some things. You're right, I need some rest and sleep. I am so lucky to have you kids, and still have children and grandchildren. I will make supper later.

Dyffryn:
I'll come and tuck you in.

William:
No, sweetheart. You stay here with your brothers, play some games together. Forget the housework, enjoy yourselves. You're just kids. Enjoy your youth. There's plenty of time to grow up, just don't grow up too quick. There are crisps, pop and chocolate in the pantry. I will see you in a couple of hours.

William leaves for the stairs, and the three watch him leave the room, all feeling very sad. Justin calms down and forgives him for what he said. He gets that he is hurting, they all are, all dealing with it in different ways. All trying to absorb what has happened and what they've gone through.

Dyffryn:
Justin, what was the forest like?

Kyle:
Tell me about the past and the battles.

Justin:
Ok. Sit down by the fire, and I'll tell you.

What Did You Think of *A Woman's Love and Protection: A Binding Contract with Life and Death*?

A big thank you for purchasing this book. It means a lot that you chose this book specifically from such a wide range on offer. I do hope you enjoyed it.

Book reviews are incredibly important for an author. All feedback helps them improve their writing for future projects and for developing this edition. If you are able to spare a few minutes to post a review on Amazon, that would be much appreciated.

Publisher Information

Rowanvale Books provides publishing services to independent authors, writers and poets all over the globe. We deliver a personal, honest and efficient service that allows authors to see their work published, while remaining in control of the process and retaining their creativity. By making publishing services available to authors in a cost-effective and ethical way, we at Rowanvale Books hope to ensure that the local, national and international community benefits from a steady stream of good quality literature.

For more information about us, our authors or our publications, please get in touch.

www.rowanvalebooks.com
info@rowanvalebooks.com